HIS FROZEN HEART

GEORGIA LE CARRE

❀ Created with Vellum

AUTHOR NOTE

Dogwood Pass is another fictional American landscape that exists only in my mind. So don't go looking for it on the map. :)

PROLOGUE

Cade

https://www.youtube.com/watch?v=MDM0yAJjlBo

I didn't lift my head from the spreadsheet I was examining even though I'd heard my wife come into the room. She shut the door with a firm click.

"What do you want, Christine?"

"I want you to fucking look at me."

I put my finger on the last figure I had just studied to mark it, and looked up at her. She had been drinking. Her cheeks were flushed. Her bee stung lips were trembling and her fists were clenched at her sides with temper. She looked like what she was. The spoiled, little rich girl whose latest whim hadn't been indulged.

We stared at each other. She bore little resemblance to the woman I married five years ago. Then she had been laughing, fresh faced, head over heels in love with me. Even her face was completely different. Since then she had allowed a slew of plastic surgeons to work on it. Pumping it with silicone, removing bits, adding bits. Until she looked like a parody of herself.

"What do you want, Christine?" I repeated.

"A man tried to pick me up on the street today."

"Did you go?"

"Fuck you," she screamed. "Why can't you be normal? Why can't you be like other husbands. They care if other men want to fuck their wives. Show some jealousy. Show me you still care." She took a step forward. "You used to think I was beautiful."

"You are beautiful," I said. Not to me, but no doubt to a lot of other men.

"I want to be beautiful to you. All I want is a bit of attention, Cade. Once you wanted me. Remember, how good it used to be between us. I was good enough for you to marry me."

"I married you because you were pregnant," I reminded coldly.

"And aren't you glad you did. Because of me you have Aria and Arron? Or would you rather I had an abortion?"

My finger lifted off the number on the page, but my expression did not change. Sometimes I wished my wife would never speak to me, because every time she did, she invariably made me dislike her more. An image of my innocent twins flashed into my mind. "What mother in her right mind would ever say something like that about her own children?"

"A mother who is desperate for some love from her husband," she cried.

"I don't love you, Christine. I never have and never will. You can go out and pretend to the world that you are the beloved wife of Cade Motenson and the mother of his children, but you don't get to pretend that I owe you a damn thing except lend you my name. You made a bargain with the devil when you decided to trick me into this sham marriage."

"You know I did it because I loved you. I still love you," she declared passionately.

"Don't waste your love on me. I'd kill it, if I were you."

"You're a heartless monster, Cade. Heartless. But I'll teach you. I'll teach you to feel pain." She whirled around and flew out of my study.

I found the number on my spreadsheet and continued breaking down the stats for the Transcorp deal. It was worth over a billion dollars. A billion I did not need, but I enjoyed the process of acquiring it. I was a confirmed workaholic Type A personality. The only rush I had left in life was from closing a massive deal, of winning.

Even before the sound of my unhappy wife's stilettos had died away in the corridor I had already forgotten about her threat. But she had not.

She made good on her promise. In a way I could never, ever have imagined.

KATRINA

https://www.youtube.com/watch?v=yTCDVfMz15M
(You gotta get up and try, try, try)

"Hey, girl!" a man's voice called.

Instantly on guard, I turned and saw a man stand from his stool at the diner counter and start walking towards me. Before starting my climb up Dogwood Pass I'd stopped for a bottle of soda and a packet of cookies at the roadside convenience store in the valley.

He slapped his thigh, as if unable to contain his excitement. "Man, I didn't think I'd ever see you again."

I could smell he'd just smoked a blunt.

"Chuck, Chuck Pearson," he supplied with a broad grin.

I frowned and looked at him blankly. I still couldn't place the face, the name, or connect the enthusiasm with a remote friendship or commonality ... which could only mean one thing. "Oh, um ..."

"You're a long way from home. How are you? What are you doing around these parts? Not living down here now, are you?" He was firing questions at me faster than I could answer.

I took a backward step. "No, I'm just passing through."

"That's a damn shame."

I smiled politely, and he scratched his jaw. "Man, what's it been? Almost two years since we last saw each other?"

He remembered me from two years ago? Wow! Life in Dogwood Pass Valley must be truly uneventful. I took another step back. "Yeah, well, I'm sorry, but I don't quite remember you."

"I guess you wouldn't," he said nodding. Then he leaned in closer to me and dropped his eyes to my breasts. "It was just that one night in Denver after all." He winked at me like he knew dirty secrets about me. I zipped up my parka to get his lecherous eyes out of there.

"Must have been someone else, Chuck. I haven't been to Denver in years."

"Naw, naw it was you. I'd recognize you anywhere, darlin'."

"Listen, I got to hit the road."

"Aw, come on. Wait around, have some cherry pie with me. They got good coffee here."

I grabbed my brown paper sack from the counter. "I really

got to go. Got to get over the pass before the snow gets too heavy."

"Well, you want me to put chains on your tires for you?" he shouted after me.

"Thanks, but I got it. I'm all good."

"Oh, I know that, Katrina. I know that." He laughed in a way that disgusted me. He was thinking about me the way he saw me in Denver.

KATRINA

My blood was boiling as I put the tire chains on. Damn men. My whole life they'd been nothing but trouble. The only way I'd crawled out of the rubble of my life was to play their game. Either way, I came out feeling broken, but hey, that's life when a girl carried the burden of a sick sister on her shoulders.

I got into my shitty car and glanced back towards the store. Chuck came out and stared at me as he swaggered towards his truck. His smile was gone.

My stomach twisted. "You better not follow me," I muttered under my breath. The bastard sat in his car leering at me. Determined not to let him rattle me, I rubbed my frozen hands together and turned my key, but of course, my ancient engine took its sweet ass time firing up. I knew he was enjoying my discomfort, but finally, my car revved and Chuck fired up his in response.

"Asshole," I cursed, my breath exhaling in a mist. Pulling out, I drove an indirect route to the highway just to see if Chuck was planning on a ride along. He was. I slammed on the gas as a light turned red leaving Chuck caught at least two cars behind me.

"Ha, ha. You stupid pig! Go your own way."

Snow fell softly as I entered the highway going over the narrow mountain pass. Dogwood was one of the most beautiful scenic drives in America, but also one of the most dangerous. Before I set off I did some research and learned it was famous for hairpin turns, overhangs and passages without a guardrail. Mistakes could cost you on Dogwood Pass.

"Snowfall is going to get heavy tonight, folks! Set your alarm clocks a little early and get those shovels ready. We're gonna get dumped on," the DJ said.

Turns out I was on a pop channel. Some teenybopper band started to croon about undying love. I scanned for classic rock stations so I didn't have to listen to their irritating jingle, but it was no use. Everything on the dial turned to static, and the radio was the height of technology in my ancient car. I switched it off.

Clunk, clunk, clunk

Damn, those chains didn't sound good. At the lookout point at the top of the pass, I pulled over. Bundling into my hat and gloves, I hopped out of the car to check the chains.

"Shit."

I didn't know much about cars, but the set on the passenger side was definitely on its last threads. If I was lucky it would get me over the pass, but I'd have to replace them as soon as I got to the valley. Not that I had money for tire chains, but no doubt, I'd figure something out. Always did.

There were a few tourists taking pictures of the vista. I chuckled at one couple that got out, took a photo as fast as they could, then ran back to their car. Like me they were freezing their asses off.

"That's it, take in the beauty," I said sarcastically, but even as the words left my lips, I realized the only things I'd actually really looked at up here were my tires. And what a pity that was. It was totally stunning. So perfectly beautiful it was hard to comprehend it was real. I took in my own moment of wonder at the majesty of the mountains.

Then, I pulled the stinging cold air deep into my lungs and wished for this spot to mark the midpoint between my old life and the new one I was dreaming of beginning. I had one job left to do, and that was it. It was only a simple thing and if I saw it to the finish line, I could pay for my sister's operation.

Once my sister was on her feet, I could start over. Change my whole life because to be honest I'd come to hate my existence that little bit more with every passing day. Now, I had one shot at the life I wanted.

What if you fail?

At least I wouldn't hate myself forever for not trying and staying stuck in the drudgery and banality my life had become.

The wind heaved a swirl of white into the air, and I looked up.

The skies were packed grey with snow that would be

descending all night. I should get going. Back in the car I took a quick glance at the map to remind myself of the whereabouts of the access road I needed. There would be no looking at the map back on the pass, all eyes on the road.

As I drove off, I noticed the freezing couple back in their parked car. They were wrapped up in each other's warmth. Something about the way they were so lost to the outside world left me strangely cold and sad.

Most of the time, I was fine with being alone. I could tell myself I was better off without love. Human beings were disloyal, greedy, ugly, shallow, selfish creatures. I didn't need them or that sappy excuse of love to hide my fear of being alone. I had seen the worst in mankind and quite frankly, no thank you.

But sometimes ...

I would see something unguarded like the couple in the car and want it. Hell, I would hurt for it. Not for the sex, although that wouldn't hurt none. I wanted someone to laugh with. Someone to protect me. I wanted that best friend I'd never had. And if he were hot too ... now that would be the icing and the cherry on the cake.

"Oh God, stop it, Katrina. You sound like a damn child. Whimpering and carrying on. Grow a pair."

I began the ascent. The road twisted up, and I fought the car against the heavy wind. The creek below was a marker for my turn. I was close. I looked down. Jesus.

"Best to look ahead or up," I told myself.

My stomach jittered from looking down at the inhospitable ravine below. One careless move and everything would be over. I stared ahead, but it didn't help. It was mostly nerves at what lay ahead of me.

A row of aspen trees blocked my view to the lower road where I'd just been. They dropped off and from the corner of my eye I saw a truck.

"Shit." I doubted myself. "It can't be."

Another hairpin twisted around. Through gaps in the trees I craned my neck to see if it was Chuck Pearson's baby-sick beige truck. In the last glimmers of daylight I couldn't be sure if it was him. I sped up all the same. A dense area of trees reached over the road concealing any remaining light and the driver behind me. I kept my speed up. The road curved around in a 'C' shape that cupped the mountain. As I came out of the bottom side, a truck exactly like Chuck's entered the top half.

"Damn vulture."

"Come on, baby. We can do this," I said, hitting the gas. The car made a grinding sound. "Ugh, why do I have such a piece of shit car?"

I put a larger gap between us. After a hairpin into another section of dense trees, I noticed that the day was turning quickly into night. His headlights were still hovering behind me. I couldn't let him see me turn off onto the access road coming up so I floored it just before taking a hard turn.

I gripped the wheel to keep control of the car, but I took that turn too fast. It snapped the passenger side chains off causing my tires to slip off the road. I fought the wheel to pull it back up, but it was sheer naivety on my part. I had already completely lost control. I was hitting every tree on that side of the mountain.

It's funny what you think about in those moments of not knowing if you're going to die. The car bounced about like a matchbox, and all around me were monstrous noises, but I didn't even scream.

Time had slowed down.

As the car hurtled towards a massive tree, nothing mattered anymore. Absolutely nothing mattered. Nothing I'd ever done wrong in the past, nothing I'd been dreaming of doing. My dreams, my goals, it all went in a fraction of a second that felt like a million years long.

For the first moment in my life, I didn't worry about anything. My sister. How I'd find the money for her. What I was going to do next. It was almost a sense of relief. The responsibility had been taken off my shoulders. There was nothing I could do to change what was happening, or anything that had happened before.

If it all disappeared into the blackness it was OK with me.

My life was shit anyway.

CADE

There was nothing in the world except the fire crackling in the wood stove, the snow falling quietly outside my window, and me sharpening my axe. Until a monstrous sound suddenly shattered the air. It reached into me like an invisible entity. My head jerked up, my body became still as I listened to it sweep over the forest air.

I had a split-second flashback.

The sight of jagged metal wrapped around still-warm human flesh. White bone broken and protruding obscenely out of human flesh, crimson blood gushing, dripping, spreading. Human flesh I had loved. The memory was etched into my cells forever. I couldn't forget no matter how much I tried.

Branches continued to snap and metal screeched together monstrously. Without thinking I was on my feet. The axe clanked on the floor. I flung open the door, and ran blindly in the direction of the sound. I'd done this before. Run in the direction of horror.

Was I crazy?

I had hidden out here to get away from the nightmare and here I was running right back to it. My boots pounded the icy ground and hit a slippery patch. I steadied myself, jumped off the frozen track, and continued on the virgin snow. Hurdling over snow-covered fallen trees and brush, I hurried down the mountain in the last slivers of daylight.

It never ceased to amaze me how life could change in an instant. A moment ago I was relaxed by the fire, the sound of my axe lulling me into an almost dreamlike state while big, soft snowflakes fell over the creek.

Now my lungs were pinched from running in the thin air, and my blood ran cold with the fear of what I might find. I knew what the piercing sound was. Will the past, the demon I've been running from for two years, sink its teeth into my flesh, and pull me under again?

I pulled myself over a boulder, and scanned the area. It was difficult to see now that the last of the sun had slipped behind the mountain, but fifty feet ahead of me, just below Dogwood Pass, a car was wedged into some aspen trees. Oh fuck! I forced myself to get closer.

Please, don't let there be kids in there.

Through the window I saw long golden hair spilling over the inflated airbag. She was alone and obviously unconscious. My heart was pounding hard as I ripped the door open and gently pulled her away from the airbag. She had a small gash above her eyebrow, but even in the circumstances it was impossible not to notice in fading light how beautiful she was.

I put my fingers to her neck to check for a pulse. It was strong ... and her skin felt warm and silky.

It was cold and snowfall was growing heavier. She was bleeding. Responsibility for some stranger was the last thing on earth I needed, but I had no choice but to take her back to my cabin and lay her by the fire. When she came to I'd explain what happened and drive her into town tomorrow. And that would be the end of the matter. My life need not change in the slightest.

I would just be doing the decent thing.

It was not like I had a choice, anyway.

I unhooked her seatbelt, slipped one hand around her back, the other under her knees, and scooped her out of the car. She was slender, but I still felt her soft curves press into me. It'd been so damn long since I'd held a woman this close.

CADE

My heart was pounding hard as I kicked open the door to my cabin. There was nothing fancy like a couch. She'd have to make do with the floor. I laid her down on the rug in front of the wood-burning stove, and pushed an old cushion under her head. Then, I found some blankets in a wooden box and wrapped them around her. Her hair lay across her face like silky gold strands. For a second I hesitated, then I smoothed it back to reveal her features. In the firelight, they were soft and delicate. Her mouth looked like it'd been dropped lightly on her face like a cherry on whipped cream.

I began to stir in a ravenous way.

Like a wild wolf.

Hardly surprising, given I had been without a woman for two years, but even so. Disgusted at myself, I jumped up and moved away from her. Restlessly, I put a log in the wood burner and looked around for a way to occupy myself. I filled the whistling kettle with fresh water and put it on the gas stove. Blowing out the matchstick, I turned to look at her. She had not moved at all. The sight of a woman, such a beautiful woman in my one room cabin, was stifling. Agitated, I rubbed the back of my neck. I need something to do with my hands. I returned to finishing my work sharpening the rest of my knives for tomorrow.

But I couldn't concentrate.

I thought about the lumpy old cushion I had shoved under her head. It probably stank of smoke. I let my knife drop to the floor and climbing the ladder to the bed above us, I snatched my pillow. I lifted her head and placed the pillow beneath it. Her hair was threaded through my fingers. I gazed down at it in horror.

Fuck, I didn't want to let go.

I forced myself to release her, and go back to my knives and sharpening block.

Out here by myself, I could completely lose myself to the rhythm of the blades as soon as I found a good flow on the straight blade. For some strange reason, the scrape of the blade against stone was not sinister, but incredibly satisfying.

Today the zen-like peace from sharpening my knives was nowhere to be found.

Instead the tangled rope of desire and restlessness inside me grew. Hell, I wanted her to wake up so I could take off her clothes piece by piece and run my hands down the inside of her curvy thighs ...

"Damn."

I turned away from her and sharpened harder. Straight

blades need a figure of eight motion over the stone. Back and forth, forward around and back, I built up faster and faster. A thought of her flashed into my head, it tripped my concentration. The knife slipped and cut me. My own blood welling up was enough to jolt me out of my uneasy trance. The kettle started whistling. Before I could go to it, the wide-eyed blonde sat up, alarmed. Her enormous eyes were trained on me. They were the most amazing color, emerald green.

We stared at each other for a long unreal moment. Awake she was so fucking beautiful, it robbed me speechless. She looked like what I imagined an angel would look like. Long blonde hair, huge green eyes, heart-shaped face. Then, I remembered myself. I dropped my knife on the floor and went across to take the kettle off the stove. A clothesline ran across the cabin above my head. I reached up and took down a t-shirt with holes in it and ripped a strip off it. I wadded up and pressed over the gash in my hand.

"Hey," I said.

She stared at me silently.

"You crashed your car. You ... got a cut on your head."

Her mouth parted slightly, but she didn't say anything. Just kept looking at me with those big green eyes. The old feelings and emotions of my life as it was before the accident came flooding back to me. I was never good at showing tenderness. I felt it, but it got locked up somewhere in my chest and never came out. I went to the cupboard in the kitchen area for the first aid kit and knelt down by her side.

"You speak English?"

She looked at the kit then back up to my face and finally nodded.

"You do know who you are and all that? Where you came from?"

She nodded again.

I tore another strip off the old T-shirt. "You want me to boil this up so you can clean your wound?"

She shook her head and I handed the strip to her. She took it from me and put it straight to her head.

Fortunately, it was only a scratch, but she winced in pain. "Argh!"

I stepped to the window. Snow was falling hard. Heavy snow and strong winds meant we were not going anywhere tomorrow, and unless it stopped, the days after either. Which was very bad news.

The cabin was already full of my desire for her. I didn't know what to say, how to talk to her. Yes, I was out of practice, but I was never good with women in the first place. I had very limited uses for them. All of them without exception ended up hating me with a passion matched only by their professed love earlier.

Even my wife.

I didn't turn around to look at her, but I could feel her gaze, smell her body. I wrapped the make-shift bandage around my cut and tied it with the help of my teeth. I looked up and saw the reflection of her hair shining like spun gold in the glass pane. Our eyes met. She shouldn't be in this cabin. I could feel my lust squeezing at my chest.

She bit her lip.

I averted my eyes and sat down opposite her on a wooden stool. I took my knife back up. "Where you headed? You got anybody who's going to be looking out for you?"

She looked startled, like she was wondering if I was an axe murderer or something.

I frowned. "Look, I don't mean you any harm. Your car is wedged between some aspens. You won't be driving out of here tonight in it. I'm just saying, with the weather coming down like it is, there's no way you can get anybody to come out and tow your car, especially on Dogwood. They've probably closed the road by now anyway. You'll have to stay here at the very least until morning."

She looked like she understood what I said, but still she said nothing. I went back to my sharpening stool.

"What's your name?"

Her voice startled me. I expected when she finally spoke that she would have a quiet voice, sweet like the angel of my imagination, but it wasn't. It was gravelly and rolled over her lips in a seductive tone. I was put off guard. "What?"

"I said, what's your name?"

"Cade."

"Oh." She nudged at the corner of a blanket on the floor with her boot.

"There something wrong with the name Cade?"

"No, no it's good. I like it. It's just not the name I would expect a burly, bearded mountain man, living alone in a cabin to be called." She smiled at me suddenly, and a deep laugh tumbled out of her. It was luscious, without an ounce of phoniness to it. It did things to me. I'd been too long on the mountain if a woman's laugh could tie me up in knots like this. I turned away from her. "What sort of name are mountain men supposed to have?"

"I don't know, Grizzly, Jedediah, Something like that?"

"I don't. Just Cade." I was struggling to be near her so I stood and went out on the front porch. I needed the biting, cold air. A few steps away I kicked at the stack of wood. An unwanted thought popped into my head. I should have left her there for someone else to find and keep overnight. There were other men living on this mountain. They would have heard the car crash too.

This was dangerous for me. I needed to be alone; to be far away so I couldn't hurt anyone else. I didn't need this complication. The weird thing was I liked her already, and I didn't want to like anyone.

Everything was fine, or rather becoming closer to fine, but now she was here I was in danger of everything going wrong again. It's just one night, I told myself. I would find a way to send her away tomorrow. Somehow.

"My name's Katrina."

I turned to see her standing behind me, wrapped in blankets, her hair draped around her. She was stunning. Fuck it. I couldn't take this for much longer.

"I'll drive you into town in the morning."

Something flashed across her eyes. As if my rejection had hurt her. "Aren't you going to make fun of my name too?"

"No." I turned away from her. I couldn't stand to look at her. I wanted to consume her, drink her in. I wanted to let my eyes fall all over her flesh and discover every inch of her with my hands, my lips, my cock. "I'll find a way to get you into town tomorrow. You can get a signal there. Call somebody to come help you."

"There's no one expecting me. No one will miss me for a while."

"I find that hard to believe," I mumbled. I hoped she didn't hear me. I sounded like a fool. "Look, if you're hungry I've got some soup. Some jerky. Not much else. I don't do a lot of cooking."

"Soup sounds good. Can I help? I feel bad you're having to go to all this trouble for me."

"I didn't intend to make it myself. If you want some soup you can heat it up yourself. It's in the cupboard."

She looked at the old wooden table where I normally prepared food, then at the cupboard. "Well, what about you? Aren't you hungry?"

"No." I know I'm an asshole.

Silence grew between us. It was like an impenetrable wall.

She looked at me with wide, hurt eyes. Then she blinked hard, as if fighting back tears. She must still be in shock. Hell, what a brute I was.

"What happened on the road?"

"My chains snapped. I lost control and went off the road. If it had been on the other side my car could have plunged off the side of the mountain. It was terrifying."

She shivered and the blanket slipped from her shoulder. My gaze fell on the curve of her neck. She pulled the blanket tighter against her.

That was precious. I was hot and she was cold. "I've got some whiskey. Want a swig?"

She laughed, that glorious, rocky laugh again. "Now you're starting to sound like a real mountain man. Yeah, I think a swig is just what I need right now."

KATRINA

"This'll warm you up." Cade handed me a shot of whiskey and took a swig straight from the bottle. A few drops dribbled down into his beard. He wiped it away with the sleeve of his flannel, checked shirt. Come to think of it, he was wearing the full mountain man uniform from head to toe, and he was wearing it well. I guess I never expected to be sitting in a cabin in the middle of the woods tonight with such a virile bear of a man, a hermit who obviously did not want my company. A fact I found unexpectedly attractive.

Our eyes met and I dropped my gaze to his hands. They were rough and weathered, covered in little nicks and cuts. I liked how they pulled through his beard straightening it every now and again, or how his hands, strong but relaxed, fell to rest on his knee, or brush over his strong chest.

"You want some more?"

"No, thanks. I don't want to get drunk and stupid. Just a little to make my head hurt less and warm my bones."

Cade grunted, then put another log in the stove. I watched

him move, sure and assured and felt a slight flutter in my stomach. This was crazy. It must have been the hit to my head. The last thing I remembered was being in the middle of nowhere and trying to outrun Chuck-pervert-Pearson, but here I was with this gorgeous, enormously sexy, mountain man, who didn't seem to like the idea of sharing his space with me.

All I could think of was sliding my body over his. I actually wanted to grip onto his back and feel the bulge of his muscles, how wide and warm he was. Then I wanted him to lay me down by the fire and take pleasure in my body again and again. I wanted to see how strong he was as he moved inside my body. And I was *never* like that with men. Ever. Usually, I detested them, their hungry eyes, and their cheating ways.

But with him?

I just wanted to bring him back to the land of the living, to show him all he was missing by marooning himself up here all alone on this inhospitable mountain. I want to … Yes, yes, I was definitely suffering the effects of some sort of concussion.

"There's a can opener in that drawer right there."

"What?" I blushed crimson.

"The soup," he reminded, his brow furrowing.

"Oh. Oh yeah, well … if you're not eating, I don't want to." I looked at him surreptitiously. Had I made my attraction obvious by the way I had stared at him? I checked my lip for drool. All good there, but it was a good thing I was under a layer of blanket because my nipples felt like they were hard enough to show through my parka. He had me aching.

"Fine. I'll eat with you," he decided, with a resigned sigh.

Dropping the blankets down on the floor, I noticed Cade looking at me then. I touched my hair and wondered if he thought I was attractive. Lots of guys did, but I wanted him to find me more than attractive. I wanted him to feel an undeniable urge to ravish me. The same crazy urge he aroused in me. I took my boots off by the door and hung my coat next to his. Then, I adjusted my big, chunky sweater over my hips and pulled at my leggings while he watched me. I couldn't help it, my movements were deliberately sensuous.

"I'll make the soup," he said curtly.

"Well, let me help."

"I said I'd make it."

An awkward silence wedged between us. I didn't know where to put myself. There was nowhere else to go in the one room cabin, apart from a level above, which you accessed by climbing a ladder. From where I stood I could see that it appeared to have only a mattress and no room for anything else. If you rolled out of bed in the night you would end up on the ground floor.

KATRINA

https://www.youtube.com/watch?v=Lj6Y6JCu-l4

I watched him open cans of Campbell tomato soup and pour them into a pan with a blackened bottom. By the time the warm familiar smell filled the small space I couldn't take the silence any longer.

"So, I guess I never said 'thank you.' For getting me out of the car."

He kept his back to me filling soup into two enamel bowls and didn't say anything.

I took a deep breath. I might as well try to squeeze blood out of stone. "So, thank you. I guess I would have frozen out there."

"Here." He handed me a bowl and a hunk of dry bread and sat on his stool. I looked around for another chair.

"I don't do a lot of entertaining," he said. "Do you want to sit here?"

"No, no, I'm fine. I'll just sit on the floor."

He grunted and turned his attention back to his food.

"So, I guess you prefer being out here by yourself?"

"Yup."

"Do you ever have people come to visit you here? Old buddies, friends?"

"No."

"No one? Not even family?"

He said nothing.

"Have you got any family?" I asked, dipping my stale bread into the soup.

He didn't answer but lowered his eyes to me. That's when I noticed how unusual they were, hazel with golden flecks in them. He put his empty bowl down on the floor and stared at me coldly. "Don't you know it's rude to pry?"

I swallowed the food in my mouth. "Well, excuse me. Don't you know it's rude to make your guest feel unwelcome?"

"You are not my guest."

He was right. I hadn't been invited, but I couldn't help feeling wounded by what he said. I wanted him to want me here. I turned the hurt into anger. There was no need for such behavior. I was taking a little too much of his shit. I put my bowl down and jumped up.

"No, I'm not your guest. No, I wasn't invited here, but I was brought here against my will. While I was unconscious! How do I know you didn't club me over the head with a tree branch ... and ... and drag me here like some Neanderthal caveman so you can enjoy the pleasures of a woman while you live out your mountain man fantasy?" I fumed, but even as the words left my lips they sounded ridiculous.

He stared at me incredulously. "You crashed your car. You were unconscious. What the fuck was I supposed to do? Leave you in the snow to freeze to death? And I assure you this is definitely *not* my fantasy. If you think you're being held here against your will, then please, walk out. Go on, it will be my pleasure."

Asshole. He didn't need to be that categoric and absolute. Now I was beginning to actively dislike him. My hands balled into fists of frustration.

"Are you kidding?" I yelled. "There are bears, mountain lions, and God knows whatever else out there, not to mention the snow storm coming down if you hadn't noticed."

"I have noticed. So, sit down, shut up, and stop making so much damn noise."

We were both silent again. I think I was shocked that I had initiated such a heated and unreasonable argument given my circumstances. I kept thinking if my rescuer had been a little old man or a woman, I would have been totally different. I would have been grateful and polite, and been more than willing to sit quietly without disturbing them until morning came. It was just that he was so sexy, so beautiful, with his chiseled cheekbones, his gorgeous eyes and his aloof, masculine manner that I wanted to know him and for him to know me. And when he made it obvious he didn't want any such thing I couldn't help needling him for a reaction, even if it was only anger.

"You'll have to sleep on the floor," he said curtly.

"Yeah, okay. I noticed you only have one bed so I figured I'd be bunking on the floor." I couldn't help the sarcasm in my voice.

His eyes narrowed dangerously. "Why? Do you think I should give you my bed?"

"No, that's not what I meant," I backtracked. I should learn to hold my tongue around him, or I was just going to make this so much harder.

"You think I should be chivalrous or something?"

"Well ..."

"Now you're having a fantasy."

"Look, I'm fine with the floor. I don't need you to do anything. You're the one that thinks you're some hero, saving me from the frozen wild of my car."

"Let me tell you something, Blondie, none of this would have happened if you hadn't been driving too fast over the pass. If you snapped your chains you must have been driving like a bat out of hell. What were you thinking?"

I sighed, embarrassed to tell him about the sleaze-ball on my tail.

He shook his head disgustedly.

"I had to speed up, okay? There was this guy—"

"Oh, here we go. There's always a guy."

"He was following me," I flared up.

"God, I wish I'd left you in that car. Now, I'm going to have some love-sick fool who's been tracking your scent busting in here. If you're thinking of making your boyfriend jealous, be warned I am not playing along."

"He's not my boyfriend."

"Well, whatever he is to you." His voice had become hard and disinterested.

"He's nothing. He's just some guy who thought he knew me. He was following me like a creep. He scared me, actually. I was trying to get away." I brushed a tear off of my face before he noticed I was crying. "I don't, um... I don't have a boyfriend anyway, since you asked."

"I didn't."

"Well, no you didn't. You assumed. I'm just correcting you."

He didn't counter offer the information, but looking at his surroundings it was pretty clear I was the only human interaction he'd had, male or female, for a while. He ruffled the hair at the back of his head. I had to force myself to look away from him, so that I wouldn't stare. The simple way he moved was sensuous, almost like an invitation, to me. He walked to the door and opened it. A strong gust of freezing wind blew into the cabin. He propped a snow shovel just inside and secured the door against the storm.

"What's that for?"

He smiled mockingly. "In case I have to shovel snow to clear a path out the door in the morning."

"Oh."

"I'm turning in. I'll drive you into town in the morning first thing."

"Okay. Yeah, I better get some sleep too. Thanks again. You know, for helping me." "Whatever."

"Good night," I said softly.

He stopped halfway up the ladder to his bed and looked down at me. I saw in his beautiful flecked eyes that he wanted to say something more, but he must have changed his mind. Even so, I sensed the tiniest bit of tenderness surface when he said, "Good night."

I dreamed of my sister, Anna. We were in our old family home. She had climbed to the top of a rickety old tree that grew in our backyard, but she couldn't figure out how to get back down.

"Stay there! I'll come for you," I yelled, but she wouldn't listen.

She was crying and trying to find a place to put her foot. In reality, my sister uses a wheelchair, is fed through a tube, and breathes through a trach. But in my dream she was normal. Her body was not yet ravaged by illness.

"Please, just wait there for me," I begged. "I'll climb up and carry you down on my back!"

"No! You can't. We'll both fall," she cried frantically.

Suddenly there was a faraway rumbling sound. It sounded like a freight train for a moment, then it increased, and filled the air all around us. Like a tornado coming from all directions. I looked around me in fear. There was nowhere to run. The force of it made the tree Anna was in shake. My legs were frozen like they were in buckets of cement. The limbs began to drop from the tree. Anna lost her footing and tumbled down.

I bolted awake before she hit the ground. The rumbling and vibrating sound of my dream was still going on. It took me a moment to remember where I was. My breath quickened with terror and I jumped to my feet. What the hell? As quick as I was up all went quiet again. I stared around me in frightened disbelief. Moonlight reflected off the snow filled room with peaceful blue light.

"Avalanche," Cade said, from above.

My head jerked upwards. "What?"

"It's over. Go back to sleep." His voice was calm, devoid of all emotion.

Oh, my God, this is crazy. What am I doing out here?

CADE

https://www.youtube.com/watch?v=0sw54Pdh_m8

I woke up that morning with a rage going on inside. The thought of her sleeping just below me was enough to keep my blood frenzied and coursing through my body. It left me with a steaming hard on. I felt like stone. How the fuck am I ever going to get this down with her below.

I rolled over and studied her.

Her face was turned slightly towards the morning light, and she looked beautiful, like an angel, or a goddess. I could have lain there watching her forever. I should have offered my bed, but she had a way of rubbing me up the wrong way. Talking of rubbing, I was dying to relieve myself. I always slept naked and my hand fisted around my cock.

Oh, fuck it. This is bullshit.

Keeping my blankets wrapped around me, I climbed down

the ladder. Stark naked underneath two layers of wool plaid and barefoot, I paused when a floorboard creaked. She stirred and twisted beneath the blankets, leaving the gentle curve of her neck exposed.

That's it. I'm over the edge.

I turned on my heel, pulled the door open, and hurdled the thigh high snow blocking the doorway. My feet plummeted into the thick snow as I ran farther into the white wilderness. I pushed myself naked through the thick powder the whole five hundred yards from the cabin to the creek.

Ah, the joys of mountain living.

My blood was running so hot for Katrina, the freezing cold water of the creek was the only thing to cool me right down. I dropped my blankets at the bank, placed my feet on the round stones that sat a few inches below the water, and shuffled myself out. The paper-thin layer of ice cracked, and I dropped in through the hole in the ice.

Oh FUCK! Icy water lapped around my balls, and my erection subsided instantly.

The creek was just deep enough to wade through up to my chest. I splashed water with my arms out wide. Anybody would think I was crazy.

Hell, maybe I *was*.

I let a woman drive me from my warm bed to a near frozen creek first thing in the morning. It was so damn cold it was impossible to stay long. I waded back to the bank where I'd discarded my blankets, and wrapping them around me quickly, I retraced my steps back through the snow.

My plan was to go back into the cabin for some clothes, then go out to the workshop without waking her up, but when I walked in she was sitting up and in the process of pulling her sweater back over her. Her arms up in the air and her breasts were exposed. Her nipples were like pebbles. Why the hell was she not changing behind the blanket I'd thrown over the washing line running across the cabin especially for her?

I felt like I had to go back to the creek and start again.

She pulled her roll neck down from her face. My blood was racing again. I was staring at her like a deer in the headlights when I realized she was staring right back at me. Not because I'd walked in on her dressing, but because my blanket had come open. There should have been nothing to see except my balls and dick shriveled up and red with the cold, but in fact, I was already way past at half-mast. Maybe she would think it was morning wood. I gathered the blanket up around my waist and went for my jeans, T-shirt, and flannel shirt.

"You're all wet," she observed. "Where did you go?"

"A dip in the creek."

She arched a dirty-blonde eyebrow. "Jeez. You must be losing it up here all alone." A look of mischief came into her eyes. "Or maybe I should call you Ice-man."

I glared at her and she changed tack.

"I put some coffee on the stove," she said. "Hope that's ok."

I may have let out a grunt. I even felt like a fucking bear this morning.

"I can't go anywhere in the morning without having coffee first," she added conversationally.

This woman had a way of making my hackles rise. "And where do you think you're going?"

"Um … I thought you were taking me into town so that I can call someone about getting my car towed? That was the plan, right?"

Without explaining what should have been obvious to her, I went ahead and finished dressing.

"It's just … I thought you couldn't wait to get rid of me, so I figured we'd be going into town first thing this morning."

I rolled up the sleeves of my flannel shirt as I crossed over to the radio. You can't pick up much on the radio out here, but there should be enough coming through the airwaves to let the weather report explain to this city chick why she will not be going anywhere this morning.

"I don't understand. Can you just say something, please?"

I turned on the radio and adjusted the dial to find a signal.

CADE

"*Officials are warning of further avalanche danger in parts of Colorado's high country because of heavy storms bringing in an extra three feet of snow and strong winds to the mountains. Reports suggest some slides haven't run this large in twenty years. There is approximately a mile of Dogwood Pass covered over by snow. So that has been closed completely until further notice. There have been no fatalities reported so far, but avalanche watch is issued at this time as this winter storm moves into the mountains.*"

"Oh. So, I guess that means we're stuck here?" she said quietly.

"Yeah."

"Well, for how long?"

"Long as it takes."

"What about food? What are we going to eat?"

"Trout."

"Trout? Oh, my God, I cannot eat trout until we're rescued."

I found it funny to see her flustered. She'd been acting cool, like this was some kind of weird adventure she found herself on and now the reality was setting in that she would not have her modern comforts and amenities for an indefinite period of time. No Facebook, no Google, no Tinder. It was kind of funny when she wigged out.

"What are you laughing at?"

I shrugged.

"Great. Just great. I'm glad you find this situation so funny. This is not exactly what I had planned for the weekend. Stuck out in the sticks in a one room cabin with someone who has been the most unfriendly rescuer since the Beast rescued Belle."

"God help me, just my luck that I've got a damn Disney princess in my cabin. I bet that's just what you're after too. Girls like you want some kind of fairy tale romance. You go around looking for 'the one' because you think that's what you deserve, a fairy tale perfect world. Well, listen up, little girl because I can tell you right now that isn't how life works."

Her eyes had become wide as she stood there taking in everything I said. I could almost see the cracks appear across her dreams as I shone a ray of realistic light on them. I remember seeing that hope and longing in women's eyes before, yeah before it all went to hell. I never wanted to watch that again.

"You don't know anything about me," she muttered bitterly.

Then she came closer and squared up to me. She was much

smaller than me, but she had the pop of a firecracker. My cock stirred. Fuck her. She got within centimeters of me. Her green eyes were blazing. She had a passion for something, I just wasn't sure what yet.

"Don't judge me just because I'm not from here because I can tell from your voice mister ... that you aren't either. Not many lumberjack, mountain men types going around sounding like they were educated back east at an Ivy League university. So, how long have you been out here, living off trout and wiping your ass with aspen leaves? Does it make you feel like you're above everyone else just because you live off the grid? Is that it?"

OK, so she was a spunky spitfire of a princess then.

We stared hard at each other, the spunky spitfire Princess and me. I could see she wanted to scream to get something through to me. Well, I had completely different thoughts as I watched her delicious chest rise and fall.

The bubbling sound of the coffee percolator drew our attention out of the heated moment, which left a second longer could have led to either her slapping me or me kissing that delicious mouth. I wasn't sure which. She stepped away towards the kitchen and opened the cupboard door. I exhaled. I needed to calm down. We were going to be stuck in this damn space for a good few days and I had already allowed the situation to become too volatile.

"There's only one cup ... sorry," I said, trying to be less harsh with her.

"That's OK. I'll put mine in a bowl. I drink a lot of coffee. Plus, it was not so long ago that I was a student. I can drink out of anything. I guess you don't have any milk?"

"I drink it black."

"Of course, you do," she murmured, handing me the coffee cup.

We drank in silence. She was looking at the snow outside the window. I watched her lips blow the steam from the top of the bowl, and how lovely the bend of her hand was around it. In a moment that was surreal, I realized I had run away from all the trappings of civilization, but it had come looking for me.

Because, I wanted her with an intensity I had forgotten I even had. I wanted her thighs around me, her nipples in my mouth. I knew why I was so tense. It made me tense to constantly keep pushing away my all-consuming desire for her.

"I suppose when I go out to use whatever kind of toilet set up you have I will not exactly be cleaning myself up with a quilted toilet paper," she said, with a lift of her eyebrows.

"It's not aspen leaves, but it's not quilted either," I mocked.

"So when will we be rescued?"

"There won't be anyone coming out to rescue us. It doesn't work like that. It's kind of the point of living out here. I don't need anybody. Nobody worries about me, and I don't worry about anyone. Snow melts, roads get cleared, happens every year. You might as well find some way to occupy yourself for a few days."

I stood and slipped my boots on by the door.

"Hey, Cade, wait."

She came over to me by the door, pulling her hair around her to one side.

"If we're stuck here together, don't you think we should try to get along? Can't we just be nice until I'm back on the road, and then you can go back to hating, or strongly disliking me, or whatever it is that you've got going on here?" Then she stepped closer with her hand extended for a shake and a dazzling smile on her face. "Come on, what do you say? Friends?"

I didn't trust myself to touch even her hand. The rest of me might follow through with pulling her in, kissing that sexy mouth, and tasting every inch of her.

"Sure, whatever." Then I turned away and headed to my workshop before I could change my mind about being such an asshole.

KATRINA

Cade left me alone in the cabin, and walked to some kind of outbuilding that I could see from the window. He was a tough cookie to crack. I couldn't believe he didn't even accept my peace offering. The more he wanted to be alone, the more it made me want to pull him back to people, people meaning me.

Once he disappeared through the door I looked at my surroundings. The avalanche may have sounded terrifying, but the results of the storm and slides were absolutely beautiful.

Snow blanketed everything in sight in great, thick piles of glittery, whipped cream freshness. Seeing my surroundings in the daylight was a mesmerizing experience. The mountains reached up all around us protective and punishing at the same time. Cade had carved himself a picturesque nook of wilderness by the creek to live in. It was absolutely stunning. This kind of natural beauty could sway even the hardest of city slicker hearts. Even mine.

Before my parents divorced, we used to go to mountains to hike as a family, but that all felt like a lifetime ago. My sister and I were the only ones left. Life gave you no guarantees. It could even destroy true love. I saw why someone would choose to live their life out here if they wanted to be away from it all, but I would never choose to live all alone. Almost everything I had had been taken away from me, except my sister, but I would never willingly give up a connection to everyone and everything in my life just to be alone.

This beautiful scenery was making me oversentimental. I turned away from the window.

By nature, I was a doer so I didn't plan to sit around in a cabin all day waiting for snow to melt. First things first though, it was time to brace myself for the cold and check out Cade's port-a-potty set up.

Cade's cabin looked like it had been there for a hundred years or more. The outhouse definitely hadn't. It looked like it was probably the first thing he built, or at least the first thing that stayed standing up. Bits of freshly sawn wood were pierced together to form planks. They let narrow shafts of light and freezing cold air through as I sat on a wooden toilet seat.

The most revealing thing about his little, rustic john was that he had hung with twine a bouquet of dried lavender for freshness. The guy was not as tough as he put on. I laughed out loud when I saw the herbs. Truth was I liked him. He told it like it was. There was nothing smarmy about him. He projected a grizzly, salty persona, and yet, I got glimpses of tenderness and magnetism inside him. The two opposites were attracting me to him to an almost uncontrollable degree.

I tore off a few rectangles of toilet paper and cleaned myself. It was not quilted, but it was not too rough either. This was definitely the most bizarre situation I'd ever found myself in with regards to a man.

I was supposed to do this one last job and then I was throwing it all out, to start again so it didn't make any sense why I was dithering around like an idiot for that bad-tempered man. It was no wonder he was jumping into freezing creeks first thing in the morning. He probably had ice water running in his veins. I had really meant it when I tried to make 'friends' with him.

It could be because I found him to be almost pulsating with power and a tightly leased sexuality. Seeing how big and angry his cock looked this morning didn't help either.

'Get over yourself, Kat. Go be useful.' I scolded myself aloud, as I pulled my pants up.

KATRINA

I spent the rest of the morning cleaning up the cabin. Not for Cade like some kind of 1950's housewife, but because I was the one sleeping on the disgusting floor with bits of wood everywhere and dust bunny balls. The stove and coffee pot needed a good cleaning too, so I went over those. Before I knew it, I'd gone over the whole place. The cabin looked sweet and cozy with wool blankets, comfy cushions, lanterns with candles inside, and logs stacked for the fire.

At home, whenever I did a big clean I liked to leave so that I could come back later and be surprised by how nice the place looked. It was silly, I know, but it was the little things you had to enjoy.

The pale winter sun reached the highest point in the sky, so I set off for an exploration trek of the area. I wanted to fill my lungs with fresh mountain air before the snow kicked in again. I walked towards the trees and higher up the mountain.

At the back of the cabin I noticed a large boxed-in contraption. I unhooked the metal door latch, swung it open and discovered a wonderland of frozen food. There was meat, vegetables, some fruit, and even long-life milk. So it wasn't just canned soup and trout. The bare-faced liar. If he thinks we're eating another dinner of canned soup he's got another thing coming. I may have to cook it myself, but tonight we're having a feast.

The walk was pretty slow going given how deep the snow was, and the steep incline as I climbed higher. I went over boulders that would have been shoulder high but with the thick snow cover only came up to my knees. After about twenty minutes of steady walking I'd warmed up from the inside. I came to a clearing where there were very few trees. It opened up in a cut between two mountains and sloped out to a flat section. As I got closer I saw steam rising. I'd heard about people hiking these mountains in search of the two-dozen natural hot springs. This must be one of them. I felt a rush of excitement, like I'd stumbled upon a treasure. It had small boulders along the edge on the downside of the mountain. It was nature's version of an infinity pool.

I dared myself to get in. It would be absolutely freezing to stand here undressing, but it had to be absolutely glorious once I got in the water. Besides, how else am I going to take a bath today? Other than rubbing a bunch of lavender from Cade's commode all over me I wasn't going to have a chance to clean myself for the next few days. My clothes would be wet on the hike back down, but I could get them dried by the fire. The water looked really inviting.

I was going in.

I giggled to think of anyone other than a bear coming along and getting a pretty good shock to find a naked chick bobbing in the water. The layers of clothes came off as fast as I could possibly get them off. The less time I had to stand nearly naked in the biting wind the better. Coat first, sweater, then all my layers apart from my bra. I undid the laces on my winter boots and stood on one of the rocks at the edge of the hot spring pool. I peeled off my leggings, piled everything at the side, and about leapt out of my bra and panties and straight into that delicious pool.

I sunk to my shoulders and groaned with pleasure. The bottom of my hair got wet, but I laced my fingers through my hair at the back of my neck and lifted it into a knot to keep it dry. I didn't want to get wet, but it looked so inviting I just couldn't stop myself. I stood to see how deep the water was. My breasts were exposed to the air as the water hit me just across the rib cage tightening my nipples. Re-submerged, I kept myself in up to the chin and blew across the surface to push the steam along. It felt glorious, like a hot bath on a cold, cold day.

I wondered if Cade knew about this hot spring. Maybe he comes here all the time to bathe. I don't see any other shower or bath device near his cabin. His cabin may be messy, he may have the rugged, bearded, ripped and tousled look about him, but he certainly didn't smell unclean. In fact, he smelled real good. He struck me as a man who took care of himself.

My imagination stepped into the driver's seat and I gave in to a delectable fantasy. Something my libido hoped would happen. In my mind's eye he climbed straight up from the valley towards me in the pool, almost marching, not missing a beat, or wavering. Twenty feet away from me he started taking off items of clothing. He pulled off his hat first, ran his hands through his hair, then off came the flannel shirt. He dropped it as he came, still striding towards me.

My mind skipped over the part where he bent over bare-assed to the wind to take off his boots, because the thought made me laugh. I bought my focus back to his chest and chiseled bits and pieces of his stomach and chest, of which I got a sneaky peek that morning.

The laughter subsided and the sexy feeling returned with force. I imagined him sliding into the water. In over his head. My back arched at the thought of him under there. He surfaced again and flicked his head to the side to shake the water off. I imagined his hands, strong and weathered, but tidy skim over the water reaching towards me. With just his eyes and nose above the water he watched me and moved closer.

Again, he slipped underneath the water, grabbed my ankles and slid himself up my legs, across my hips, then up my torso and between my breasts, out of the water face to face. I thought about us kissing and how amazing it would feel to have his hard body pressed tight against me. My imagination took me so far away I was only brought back to reality when I realized the pressing sensation over my clitoris had come from me, and not my imaginary Cade.

My eyes snapped open. "This is ridiculous! Pull yourself together, Kat."

He's just one guy, and not a very friendly one at that. Probably misogynistic too. All the men in this whole big world and I was acting like he is literally the last man on earth. Why was I acting so crazy over him, anyway? He was rude, uncivilized, and uncommunicative, a brute. And he lied about how much food he had squirrelled away. To top everything else, flannel and beards had never been my thing. There must be something terribly wrong with me.

And then, I started to think of how that infuriating man's rough beard would feel between my legs. So help me, God. I squeezed my eyes shut as if I could stop the relentless images, and tried to pull my thoughts away from him, but instead I thought of those rough hands on my body. I thought of the rippling muscles on a sunny day when they were all tanned and glowing with sweat. They must be really beautiful.

All that wood he had stacked up on his porch. I bet he chopped it all up with his axe while he was shirtless.

My fingers found my clit again.

Oh, what the hell? Who can it hurt if I indulge in a drop of fantasy? After all, you were supposed to fantasize about things you would never do in real life. I would never fuck him in real life. Not even if he asked!

So: a fantasy was in order. And no ordinary fantasy would do either. This one had to be special ... after all, how often does a girl come a across a man such as Cade? I closed my eyes and let myself drift off ...

KATRINA

https://www.youtube.com/watch?v=FbQfE2Oi6Wo

I was polishing a table in the cabin, Cade's cabin, but a bigger more luxurious one. It had a bed downstairs and the floors were gleaming. I was feeling hot so I'd taken off all my clothes, and wearing nothing but a little French apron with very high heels and sheer black stockings, obviously. My hair was in a messy bun on top of my head.

The polish I was using smelled of lavender.

I heard Cade walk in through the front door and I turned my head around to watch him. He was shirtless and leaning against the door. All those sun-kissed, freakishly strong, and sinewy muscles were on display. His head was tipped back and underneath the coarse beard, all the thick cords in his neck stood out. He ran his hand through his longish hair and his biceps tensed and bulged.

My gaze caught the beauty of the gestures and moved down to his sculptured chest, which was swelling with muscles. The hard tissue flowed down from that chiseled perfection to where his six-pack popped. Why, his whole body was a living work of art. My eyes followed the dark happy trail lower. And lower still.

Oh my! I knew he was hard because he had a clear view of my pussy peeking between my ass cheeks. He was so beautiful and he wanted me so badly.

"Hello," I said softly, my own lust flaring in me.

He didn't answer, just walked in while unbuckling his jeans and revealing his massive cock. When he was behind me he licked the skin from my collarbone up to my ear, drawing a tortured moan from me.

"Cad ..."

"Shhh ..." he hissed, as he snaked his hand between us and ran his callused fingers along my exposed slit.

"Well, well, Katrina. You're supposed to be cleaning. Why are you so fucking wet?" he growled.

"I can't help myself," I whimpered.

"Open your legs wider," he ordered.

I obeyed.

He dropped to his knees and swiped his velvety tongue over my pussy, then he pulled on my hips, arching my back as he drove his tongue deep inside my wetness. He started licking and sucking my nectar as if he couldn't get enough.

"Oh yes. Yes," I cried out, closing my eyes tight.

But suddenly his hot ravenous mouth was gone. My lips parted in shock as he shoved two fingers into me and started fucking me with them.

"Is this what you were waiting for?" he demanded. "Is this why you're dressed like a dirty girl?"

"Fuck you," I said, but I was trembling with anticipation.

He chuckled softly and stood. I heard his jeans fall to the floor. He grabbed one of my breasts in one hand and squeezed the round globe while tugging on the nipple. I moaned with the exquisite sensation. Raking his other hand into my messy bun, he grabbed a handful of hair.

He pulled my head back at the same time that he rammed his cock into me. No condom, no protection. Nothing just his bare cock completely buried inside my pussy and his hard stomach and chest pressed tight against my back. I screamed at the invasion.

I was no virgin, but he was so well hung when he forced himself into me, I felt as if all the other men had been only boys, their penises not yet developed. With Cade, it felt as if he was ripping me apart from the inside out.

"God, you're tight," he groaned, as I bent in half and pushed my hips back against him. In that position my calves began to ache.

I could feel myself shaking uncontrollably as he kept on slamming hard and fast into me. He took his hand off my breast and pulled at my clit as he continued to drive himself deep into me. My clit throbbed wildly against his hand and I knew I couldn't last much longer.

"You wanted to feel out of control. You wanted me to take you roughly, without permission?" he snarled.

"Yes," I said, but I was almost incoherent with pleasure.

"I'm going to come," I screamed, as I began to lose control.

Then my body started to spasm and clamp down on his cock. As my body sucked and milked him, he bit down on my shoulder and fucked me ruthlessly. I felt his cock pump hot cum into me and it was the most exquisite feeling in the world ...

My heart was racing with the intensity of my climax and my skin had reached the prune stage. When I built up enough courage and braced myself against the cold, I dashed out of the water, and, no kidding, the freezing air enveloped me like an icy blanket. I felt as if the water on my body was turning to ice. Vigorously I dried myself with the exterior of my coat. Then I dressed in record time. Much faster than I had undressed. Leggings do not move well over wet skin, but I pulled them so hard, I almost ripped them.

As I crouched down to lace my boots, some movement in the trees caught my attention. It was a beautiful doe. She was sniffing around for food but not finding much. She even lifted her front legs onto a tree trunk to reach for some evergreen. Poor thing. She was probably desperate for something to eat. It was late in the winter, but there was still no sign of spring anytime soon.

Without making any jerky moves, I slowly stood, and watched her. I had never seen a deer up so close before. I studied her pretty face, her big eyes, delicate features, and her thin, graceful, but strong limbs. I wished I had thought about bringing my cell phone. I would have loved to have taken some pictures of her.

I admired her.

She made surviving the harshness of life look beautiful, simple, as though it didn't scare her. Life scared me. I was scared all of the time that this big, bad world would swallow me under, starve me out, or just take my sister away. I felt the doe's desperation, but I couldn't even begin to imagine exhibiting such grace. No, I haven't been a very good person. But I guess I did what I had to do.

The wind changed course and she startled away in the opposite direction from me. She may have caught my scent and been scared off, or more likely she had caught the scent of something bigger, with teeth more ripping than mine behind me. Instinctively, I turned around, but all was quiet.

I decided not to stick around and find out what frightened her. Now was probably a good time to get back to the cabin and see what I could rummage from Cade's freezer for dinner. I wished her luck and set off the way I had come.

CADE

The winter sun was low, so I called it a day. Not that the work I'd done warranted finishing, I just couldn't take how distracted my thoughts were anymore. All day my mind had been bombarded with thoughts of Katrina. Images I'd caught of her flashed into my brain, an exposed shoulder, her tousled hair falling down her back, the slight parting on that full mouth.

My hands were covered in little nicks and tiny cuts where my concentration had dropped to Katrina. Mostly to a naked Katrina.

The damn devil sat on my shoulder all morning and tried to tempt me to go into the cabin and chase her giggling up the ladder to my bed. In my head that's how she'd react. In reality, she'd probably turn on some of that sassy, princess spunkiness and make me work hard every inch of the way.

"What the fuck, man? You've got to get this woman out of your place. She's messing with your head."

I thought about taking her to Beau's cabin. He was too old to do anything about his erections, and he'd be grateful for the eye candy. He lived further down the valley, and it was only a couple of hours on foot, but it will probably take half-a-day for a city gal. Maybe tomorrow.

As I approached the cabin I saw the soft glow of firelight coming from inside, and when I opened the door, a wash of wonderful smells engulfed me.

"What the hell is that?" I said from the doorway.

A flash of annoyance crossed her face, but she plastered a smile on her. "Hi," she replied brightly, "I took the liberty of cooking us some dinner. I found some meat in the freezer and a bunch of vegetables, so I just threw them all together, and added some spices and oil too. Hope you like it."

It smelled delicious, and I can't remember anticipating eating a meal that much before. I wanted to say thank you, but I couldn't. It looked like she'd cleaned and tidied up the cabin too. She'd been here less than a day and already she'd made the place a more enjoyable, comforting place to live than I had in two years. In a way I loved it, and on the other hand it brought back a memory, a feeling of connection that ripped at me.

She frowned at my expression. "Sorry, but I just couldn't stand to eat a can of soup for dinner for the second night in a row. I like to eat, and I like to eat good food!"

"Cooking fancy for one is not high on my list of priorities, and no, I don't mind."

"Good." She turned to the wood-burning stove and I thought I saw the glimmer of a small smile of satisfaction curve her lips, as she turned to take out two tin foil wrapped parcels. That's when I noticed a familiar check print flannel shirt.

"I am, however wondering why you're wearing my clothes?"

"Oh, yeah!" She laughed her deep, rocky laugh, which was so sexy and self-assured it made my stomach clench. "Sorry about that. My clothes got soaking wet, so when I got back to the cabin today I just put on some of yours while mine are drying." She waved at the clothesline.

"They look good on you," I said and immediately regretted making the comment.

She didn't say thank you, but those big green eyes lit up. A sign she was reading far too much into the compliment. I scowled. It didn't matter what she thought, it would be Beau's problem by tomorrow.

"Well. They'll probably be dry in a little while. I can change out of your clothes if it's weird."

"I'd rather you change out of them as soon as yours are dry."

"Oh. OK." She looked crushed, like a kicked puppy.

"Let's just eat," I said curtly.

"Ok, yeah, I don't want this to get cold."

I grunted.

"Well, I hope this dinner is good." She opened up the two tinfoil parcels. Inside were juicy looking pieces of meat with onions, squash and tomatoes sprinkled with rosemary. She spooned rice over them, which soaked up the juices from the meat and vegetables. She put a corncob next to that, and gave me the parcel with a kitchen towel underneath to protect my hands from the heat. I grabbed a fork while she took the same for herself and sat down on the floor.

We ate quietly. After a long day of work the food was surprisingly delicious and totally kept my attention until we were almost done. Then, something she'd said earlier struck me as odd.

"What did you mean, 'when I got back to the cabin?' Where did you go?"

She wiped her mouth and grinned happily. "I just went for a walk today. There was nothing else to do all by myself, so I just took off on a little exploring expedition, and I ended up finding one of those hot spring pools people are always searching for up here. I saw some tourists buying maps for them at the store in the valley, but I'd never come across one. It was amazing. I guess you must go up there all the time. You've got your own personal hot tub up there. I did wonder if that's where you go to take a bath."

I put the fork down and stared at her. "You went all the way to the hot spring?"

CADE

"Well, it wasn't *that* far. I mean, it was a good ways walk, but it felt good."

"Do you know what could have happened to you out there by yourself?"

"Well, yeah I guess. But still, you've got to just keep your wits about you and still get out in the world. Experience life, not just stay cooped up in a little cabin away from it all. Don't you think? Or maybe I'm asking the wrong person about that."

"I don't know who you'd ask about whatever you're getting at. What I'm talking about is I don't want to have to tell the Sherriff there's a girl out here that's been killed by a bear, or ripped to shreds by a mountain lion. You are enough trouble just being out here, you'd be even more trouble to me if you're dead."

"I see. Well, that's very considerate of you to bring it to my attention. I hope you enjoyed your dinner." She wadded up her empty tin foil into a ball and tossed it to the kitchen trash can. "I'll get out of your clothes for you right now." She threw a quilt over the washing line and started undressing behind it. Okay, that was her definitely pissed.

"Damn." She let out an irritated sigh. "Would you kindly pass my clothes to me, please? They're hanging up under the balcony."

They were dry and warm. I took my time unpinning them from the line just so I could hold her things; smell them, run them between my fingers. It also gave me time to think through what to say to make up for my blunder. Talk about saying the exact opposite of what you were thinking. Here I was being driven out of my mind with desire for the woman and I was talking about how inconvenient it would be for me if she were dead. I had come across like a little boy on a playground pulling at a girl's ponytail.

"I was just worried about you out in the wild by yourself," I said gruffly, laying her sweater across the line to her. The idea of her naked, only a few inches away on the other side of a patchwork quilt, made me almost jittery with hunger for a taste of her.

"If I'd known you were out roaming around I would have come along, brought some protection."

I laid her leggings and t-shirt over the line.

"I need the rest of it," she said abruptly.

I hung her bra and panties. "I'm sorry ... I'm not the most ... well, I don't always know ... I'm sorry for being an asshole." From my side of the quilt I listened to her put on her clothes and something that sounded suspicious like a muffled sniff escape her. Shit. "If we're still snowed in tomorrow I'll go with you if you need to take a walk. OK?" Where the fuck did that come from? I was supposed to take her to Beau's. I exhaled. Maybe she can stay one more night to make up for me being such a jerk.

"Sure," she agreed, but there was a slight tremor to her voice making me feel like I still had more ground to make up in the way of an apology.

"You made dinner, I'll make us some drinks."

I walked to the cupboard and pulled out a bottle of red wine, a drink I stashed away for the moments when I needed a taste of my old city life. Then, I drank wines that cost over $2000.00 a bottle. This bottle was from the local store. Almost undrinkable. I poured it into a pan. There wasn't much left, a half of a bottle between us. I put the pan on to the stove and dropped in a bag of spices. Putting it on a low heat setting I left it to slowly warm the wine.

"I'll be right back," I called and went outside.

Putting some kindling on the fire pit I got a campfire going. It would be nice to have our wine around the fire and look at the moonlit scenery. Also, that would be a lot easier than sitting inside the cabin stewing in her scent. That would be more than I could stand. I needed to cool off physically and figuratively.

I took a couple of dry logs from inside my workshop. The ones stacked outside were too damp to start a fire easily. I thought about the fire between Katrina and I. It wanted to burn. Maybe the fire is only from my side. Maybe I've just been out here too long for my own damn good and the sight of a gorgeous woman is making me feel the warmth of flickering flames. But maybe she doesn't feel that.

"Hey," she said from the open door of the cabin. "Whatever you got cooking on the stove smells really good, but it's about to boil."

I blew underneath the flame to agitate the kindling and light the logs well and stepped back to the cabin. She stood in the doorway looking at the fire, forcing me to work around her in close contact. I came through the doorway and her chest brushed against my abs. I paused against her and saw the reflection of flames in her eyes and I felt such a burning heat inside no amount of freezing wind and snow could cool me.

She turned to me and I slipped into the cabin shaking with desire. The power she had over me was astounding.

"Yeah, let me take that off the heat. It's not supposed to boil. We don't want to burn off the alcohol," I said as coolly as I could.

"So, what is it? Surely hemlock doesn't smell that wonderful."

I ignored the jibe. "Mulled wine. Ever had it before?"

"No, never even heard of it."

"It's perfect for a snowy night like this. I thought we could have a glass or two around the fire outside. Can you handle the cold?"

"Well, I think so. As long as I'm near the fire I'll be fine."

"Here."

"Huh, a real wine glass. And you have two of them! Now, this is special! Where did you get two wine glasses from?"

I didn't answer her question and blatantly ignored her

sarcasm. I poured myself a glass of the warm, spicy wine and went out to tend to the fire.

"Oh, bring the stool," I said.

"Um, sure."

She expected me to carry it for her. The problem was I *fucking* wanted to. But being openly nice and charming will only get me into trouble. It was hard enough keeping her at an arm's distance when all I really want is to wrap them around her for the rest of this night and several after. I can't imagine ever getting my fill of the taste of her. I went to the back of the cabin and found an old stool to sit on. It was a bit shaky, but it would do.

"This is nice," she said when we were seated and sipping. "I feel privileged to be out here having this experience in the wild. I mean this is truly wild, off the grid living."

"If that's your opinion, does that mean you'll eat trout tomorrow?"

She laughed.

That got me. Her laugh is truly the most enticing laugh I've ever heard. It made me want to drop down in front of her, part her thighs, and just look at her sweet cunt. I wanted to press it warm, fleshy, and wet against my naked skin while I sucked her tongue. I wanted her to arch her back and lift her breasts to the sky so that I could lick them and listen to the sounds that escaped from her.

"Yeah, I'll eat trout if that gives me an authentic experience of living in the wild. Not that I knew I was looking for that this week, but hey, I'm here. Let's go with it."

My pants already felt tight. I pulled my crazy thoughts back to the easy conversation. "So, whatever I catch tomorrow that's what we eat."

She grinned. "Ok, it's a deal. You have some steaks in the freezer if I don't like it though, right?"

"You eat what you're given, city chick. But, yes, I have deer steak in the freezer."

"Did you just smile?" she asked. "Well, that's a first. Never seen a smile from you before. You should do it more often. It looks good on you."

I didn't answer. True, I had smiled at her. A real smile hadn't crossed my face in the last two years. I was struck by the fact. How did she make me do that? For so long I felt as if I wasn't even allowed to smile anymore. A blister of guilt popped inside me. I threw the rest of the spiced wine down me and went in for the rest of it in the pan.

"So, deer steak ..."

She filled the silence I'd let drop like a lead balloon. Once my glass was full to the brim I refilled hers too and tossed the pan in the snow still pissed off at myself for the smile.

"You know, I saw a deer when I was out hiking today, after I swam in the hot spring. You really have to come swim with me. It was glorious. I did think about you while I was up there. You know that you shouldn't miss out on what's so close to your cabin. That's all."

"You saw a deer?"

"Yeah, a doe. She spooked at something behind me, so that's when I came back down to the cabin."

"Do you know what it was?" I asked.

"I don't know. I didn't see anything and I didn't want to wait around until it showed itself. I just took that as my cue to get the hell out of there. If it's not good enough for Bambi, then I want no part of it either."

"The saying is that if there are deer around, a mountain lion is close behind. There was probably a mountain lion tracking that doe. You must have put yourself between them."

She smiled happily. "Oh well, I got out of there. That doe and I will live to see another day. No harm done."

"That's a hell of an attitude to have out here. One that will get you killed for sure. Do me a favor and don't go anywhere by yourself again. My house, my rules."

"Alright, fine." She sipped her warm wine. "How many more days do you think we'll be snowed in?"

This would be a good time to tell her she won't be staying with me, but Beau. "No telling. Snow's coming again tonight. We'll wake up to fresh lay in the morning."

"Will my car be buried?" she asked with a frown.

"Oh, I can dig it out. That's the least of our worries. It's the mountain that will be unforgiving. The mountain says when we can travel here. Her house. Her rules. I just follow them."

She grins again. A big genuine smile that would melt any man's heart. "Ok, I get it. I won't go off by myself again. It'll be more fun if you go with me anyway."

Fun? It's been a long time since I heard or used that word. I just don't know if I'm ready for fun yet. Especially with her.

KATRINA

I woke up in the morning feeling like I was made of lead from a terrible night's sleep. The cabin was empty. Cade must have gone fishing to catch our trout breakfast. It can't taste that bad, can it? I put my clothes back on.

Before going to bed, all by myself, I had undressed with faint hope I would have a visitor to my pallet on the floor. But somewhere in the night, my hope of a real man's moving body on mine died, and turned to my usual habit of running through my list of worries and adding a few extra ones I never knew I had.

I put the coffee on and looked out of the window.

Outside were the stark reminders of our evening together. What had seemed like a romantic interlude in the night looked very different in the cold light of day. The pan Cade had tossed aside was covered by fresh inches of snow so only the handle jutted out, the stools sat too wide apart for coziness, the extinguished embers by a pile of wet snow gave the scene a look of desolation rather than romance.

I didn't know where it all went wrong last night. Things were going well, or so I thought. He got intense for a while, then he went into his own mind, and climbed up to his bed never saying a word.

Not that it stopped me from hoping and waiting. I think I was restless and unable to sleep from being near him. I couldn't stop thinking about how his hardness had brushed against my breasts. The way my nipples had instantly become hard. God, I wanted him so much.

For ages I lay there and thought about Cade. For the other half of the night I wrestled with the 'What do I do about my sister' question. Would there be enough for her so I can start fresh again? I worried that life will be like this until the day I die, a rat race just trying to make enough money for my sister and I to keep the wolves at bay. Will there ever be a day of peace when I can stop worrying? Someday will I have plenty? Will my sister make it to see that day?

My mind raced with scenarios. Get rich quick schemes and jobs morally beneath me played out in my head, tempting me.

Then, finally, when I could put it off no longer I wondered about the scheme I'd already taken part in and if the low laying morals to them will haunt me forever. In the early hours of the morning I exhausted myself enough to fall asleep.

I pulled on my coat and boots and went outside.

A few inches more snow had fallen in the night, but not much difference considering how much there was already on the ground. However, it was the look of the weather that morning that made it seem almost ominous. It was foggy and damp and the air felt oppressive and eerie.

I didn't like it.

I pulled the pan out of the snow, dusted the stools, and brought them all back inside the cabin. The coffee wasn't going to drink itself, so I poured myself a cup. The hot liquid felt like heaven. *Please, God, let that snow clear before we run out of coffee.*

Cade had been gone for a long time. I was hoping to drink the coffee with him. Then, I had the bright idea to take him a flask of coffee down to the creek. Maybe by the time I get there he'll have caught this trout. I filled a flask of black coffee and opened the front door.

From the porch, I saw Cade's boot tracks in the snow leading towards the creek. He told me last night it wasn't a great distance away, around a bend through the trees and down to the water. I followed his footsteps, adjusting my stride to match his large boot prints. I laughed at myself as I mimicked him. Cade has a sexy, self-assured walk. Although, I was not sure it looked so good on me.

By the time I made it to the creek, he wasn't there. I looked up and down the bank for him in surprise. His footsteps didn't go anywhere else. Just went straight into the freezing water, and even though I knew he took a dip in the creek, it still sounded just plain crazy. Why would anyone willingly wade into the ice-cold water? The creek was beautiful though, and made a sound so peaceful you could almost feel the tones massaging your worries away.

OK, so he obviously didn't go fishing this morning. I guess he thinks we'll be eating another can of soup for dinner.

Wrong. Before walking back towards the cabin, I took off a glove and put my hand over one of the small, round, stones about the size of my palm. The water pushed over and around my hand in such a calming way. Still, it was freezing, almost literally, and I'd take the hike to the hot spring for a bath over the breathtaking cold of the creek anytime.

I trekked back through the snow retracing my tracks. As I got closer to the cabin I heard a sound coming from the outbuilding a stone's throw away. It was a square building that sat some distance away from the cabin, and without the snow I would have spotted it earlier. Stacked neatly outside the door were cut sections of a tree trunk, some in the shape of discs, some longer pieces and logs. I don't know why I didn't think he might have been there. I veered off the path and started walking towards it instead.

The door was ajar wide enough for me to peek through. There were worktops on both sides, like a galley. There were also many windows on all sides. I was no Peeping Tom and I hadn't intended to spy on him. I had planned on announcing my presence and going in, but I was just so struck by the sight of him so completely lost in the wood structure he was making that I couldn't stop looking. I loved the way his tall, muscular frame moved around the wood, like he was wrapping himself around it, protecting it, pushing and pulling at it, as if he was giving it life with his own body. Almost as if he was birthing it.

The piece he was working was fastened in place on top of a pedestal, and he was using a chisel and a wooden mallet to gauge out sections. As the wood shavings fell away, he swiped his powerful hand over the ridges and grooves that swirled and curved like water in the wood. His fingers trailed and lingered, as if he was caressing the wood, as if he was asking it to tell him tales of the life it had weathered, of storms and strong winds, and the animals it had sheltered. His movements were as sensuous as a panther prowling to the river at dusk. I heard nothing, but maybe it spoke to him. His attention in his creation was so total.

Oblivious to my prying eyes, he squinted at the sculpture. Then he placed his chisel on a pale spot, raised his mallet into the air and let it fall. The blade dragged through the wood.

Mesmerized, I watched his face as he leaned in to see the effect of his action. How different he was. There was purpose, determination, hardness, mystery, and sheer beauty shining in his face.

Grasping the edges of the platform the sculpture was standing on, he shifted it around so he could work on the other side of it. That was when I saw the other side. It was the bust of a woman. The lines he was following down the back were the locks of tussled, uneven hair.

Her face was still rough and unfinished, but in a way it was more beautiful than what it would be finished. I saw the raw power of his genius. I was stunned that he had brought it to its current, intricate state from being a log like the ones carelessly stacked just outside the door.

I watched him for ages. It was only when Cade stopped to wipe the sweat from his brow with his sleeve that he spotted me in the doorway.

KATRINA

"What are you doing?" he snapped, the expression on his face changing instantly.

I pushed the door open, making it creak, then I entered his workroom. "I'm sorry, I didn't mean to spy! I just didn't want to barge in on you. You looked busy."

"I *am* busy."

"Can I see? It's beautiful. You're really talented."

"No, it's not finished."

I ignored him and got around on the other side so I could see the face properly. I wanted to see the object of his crazed attention. A surge of jealousy motivated me as I imagined who this woman might be who captivated Cade's creative energy so absolutely she made him work like a man obsessed. I turned the pedestal slightly, ran my thumb over the cheek. The wood was cool and smooth under my hand and I could smell the fragrance of the wood. It swirled around the pale sculpture like an invisible ghost. Suddenly, I knew what I was touching.

"Damn it, Katrina. You shouldn't even be here. I don't want anyone disturbing me here."

His harsh voice ricocheted around the room, bouncing off the walls, but I didn't turn towards him. My voice was only a whisper that misted in the cold air of his workshop. "It's me, isn't it?"

There was a pause too long to make whatever he said next truthful. "Of course not. You are the most vain person I've ever met. Just because the carving is of a pretty face, you think it's you?"

My head whirled around. "Of course, it's me! Come on, I mean, this looks exactly like my face, and that is totally my hair! It's got to be me."

"Sorry." He shrugged his shoulders. "Get over yourself. It's not you. Now, I'm actually trying to work so if you don't mind can you get out of my workshop?"

"Jeez, you are such a rude pig." I turned to go, but said over my shoulder, "I don't believe you though. That's me. Even if you don't realize it's me yet."

He stared at me without smiling. "Can you please leave?"

I started to go and then remembered our discussion from the night before. "It's just that last night you said you were going to catch us a trout. I thought you had gone fishing when I woke up this morning. I got up and found you'd gone. I went down to the creek, but you weren't there."

"Did you expect me to wake you up before I left?"

"Well, no, but it would have been nice to know where you were."

His eyes widened. "You think I need to tell you where I'm going. What is that? So you don't *worry* about me? Seriously?"

"Yeah," I shot right back at him. "Is that so hard to believe that I want to know where you are for your safety?"

He shook his head in disgust. "Are you trying to play house with me? Why are you so concerned with having every meal together, waking up together? What the hell is this about?"

"It's not about anything! It's just so I won't worry about you."

"Listen, I don't need anybody worrying about me. You don't even know me, so what the hell do you care?"

"Humph. Seems last night you were pretty worried about me going to the hot springs and getting myself into trouble. You were worried about me. You don't even know me!"

"We're just waiting for the snow to melt and then we can get you out of here forever. Once you're gone, you'll never think about me and nor will I think of you."

I felt small and foolish. I'd let my lust for this guy reduce me to a desperate, hot mess. This was obviously a classic case of he's-just-not-that-into-you, and I should have recognized that before I made such an absolute fool of myself. The signs were all there, especially this morning. What an idiot I've been. I felt so ashamed I just wanted to be alone and be as far away from him as I could.

KATRINA

I ran from Cade's sawdust covered floor workshop, past the cabin, the campfire and snowed under truck and headed down the mountain to where I thought my car might be still. I ran out of embarrassment. A fresh surge of shame hit me as I remember how sure I'd been the woman he was sculpting was me. I don't know why I thought that. Her face was not even finished. I'd been falling all over this guy, dripping with sweetness and stinking of desperation ever since I arrived. I'd never done that with anyone before and it hurt to be so soundly rejected.

I needed to get a grip. He was just a guy.

The wet, heavy snow made it exhausting to move through. Mist hung not far up ahead. But I wouldn't give up and turn around. I slogged on through, shame pushing me farther down the mountain. I just wanted to get down there, by myself with no one coming to my aid. I'd always taken care of myself before and I didn't need him or anybody else to save me.

Sure he rescued me that time, but he did it because he had no choice. And ever since then, at every turn he made it crystal clear I was not wanted, and yet I kept on trying to get him to like me. It was pathetic.

I followed my instincts over boulders in the direction of where my car should be on the closed off Dogwood Pass. Unfortunately, my instincts were not exactly sharp as a tack. My car was out there somewhere, probably still wedged between some trees and covered in fresh snow, but it was about as good as invisible to me. Actually, I was beginning to realize I couldn't find my way anywhere in the eternal white that surrounded me.

Exhausted and disoriented, I sat on a stone and rested my back against a cluster of boulders behind me. Suddenly, emotion crept in on me. I felt utterly defeated. I had gone about it all in the wrong way. I had tried too hard to seduce him and I had failed. Tears, cold on my face, sent a shiver down me. I felt silly for crying, but what the hell was I going to do? I was stuck in a ridiculous situation.

He didn't want me and even though I, too, had enough and wanted out of this situation, I couldn't. The fact was I couldn't get out until the snow cleared away some. Once it did, I would leave and go straight back to my sister. I buried my face in my hands. But with no money, how will I pay for her medical bills?

I need money. I have to survive and get the money for her. Somehow, I must find a way to get my hands on it.

I looked around me.

It was so beautiful, but I could enjoy none of it. I stifled a sob.

I was not beaten yet. I was never one for giving up. I would try again. I decided to march myself back up that mountain to Cade's cabin and exist peacefully alongside him. Both of us would be equally disinterested in each other until the snow clears and then I would get out. It was so cold my tears cooled on my skin.

I stood up, brushed my tears away from my face and set off back through the fog.

The next moments came so fast, it was hard to believe they happened at all. It was like the memory of it that lives in my mind became more real to me that when it occurred in real time. It began when my boot slipped in the wet, slushy snow. I slid down for what felt like ages, my body hitting on everything hard and stony for about thirty feet. When I came to a stop, I was all arms and legs in every direction. Before I even took a breath, I sensed the presence of someone, something.

Oh shit!

The strength of her stare was palpable. I knew I should move, try to scare her away, yell or jump around, throw a stone or something, but I didn't. I froze. With a strange mixture of fear, shock and awe, I stared into her yellow eyes.

She was a magnificent golden creature. It was like seeing royalty. Out here she was the Queen with a stunning, angular face, enormous fluffy paws, and eyes that knew what power they commanded. Almost flirtatiously she flicked her tail, which seemed to be as long as her body itself and was thicker than I expected it to be.

I'd never seen a mountain lion this close.

She must have only been about fifty feet away. She was

downhill on the mountain from me, standing crouched, poised to sprint, and listening. I bet she could hear my heart beating in my chest, smell the scent that emanated from me. She moved with prowess from one boulder to another, graceful, sure-footed and watching me the whole time. I could see that she was giving herself a better vantage point to track me from.

I had to do something, but I didn't know what.

Her coat was thick and luxurious and her strength was evident in her sleek muscles. There would be nothing I could do if she attacked even on my strongest day, much less banged up from a fall. Not that I could feel any pain at all. It was delayed by shock. Some part of my brain noted that if she got me in her jaw I probably wouldn't even feel the pain.

It was in that moment I decided I had to move, but I realized that wasn't going to be so easy. Time had shifted to slow motion. I threw my legs under me and fell over immediately.

A searing pain came from my knee.

Oh, I felt that. Fear filled me and replaced the awe I had felt for the mountain lion with sheer panic. She smelled it in me. I saw the change in her gait. She was approaching faster. She knew now that she had the upper hand.

Again, I tried to stand, with every cell in my body screaming with pure, unadulterated fear. In those few seconds I thought about my parents. How sad they would have been to know I would find my end in a mountain lion's belly. I thought of Cade and how he tried to warn me, but I was so stupid I did not take heed. In those seconds I even felt sadness that Cade and I would never know each other.

Then I thought of my sister. What would happen to her without me?

I had to find the will to fight for my life.

A fearful guttural sound came out of me as I attempted to scare her away with my voice. She shamed me with a roar like I have never heard in my life. So ferocious and wild. The still mountain air amplified it. This was no cuddly big cat. She was a meat eating, killing machine, and I was her winter score to ensure her survival and see another spring.

On one leg, I leaned for a stick just out of reach and tossed it like a Frisbee towards her before stumbling again. It seemed to distract her away from her poised attack position long enough for me to reach another stick and a rock. I threw them one at a time. The lion moved to another boulder on an even level to me and looked at me unblinkingly. As if she was wondering why I was prolonging the inevitable. She gave the impression she was in for the long haul. Both of us knew, eventually, I would run out of things to throw at her.

I yelled again and hopped on one leg. I thought of Anna again. Only her. I thought of how she would be alone in this world and the painful death she would have. This just couldn't happen. Not yet. I promised my parents to take care of her. This wasn't my moment to die. I'd fight this lion with my bare hands if I had to.

Her paws thudded when they hit the snow.

The sound was petrifying. It filled my entire body. Then, I heard the thudding sound coming from behind me. I turned just as Cade reached the back of me. He picked me up by the waist and lifted me in the air yelling all the while. The lion ran to within fifteen feet of me, her eyes never straying from mine.

She was furious.

CADE

The lion got closer.

I'd prepared myself for an encounter like this, but I'd never had one this intimate before. I watched the lion to read every twitch, eye movement, and breath she took.

"Raise your arms up high! Make noise!"

Katrina stretched her arms out high and yelled.

I shouted and stomped around out wide to make us seem like a large figure to the lion. If she feels that you're much bigger than her she won't bother you.

"Arms out wide!"

The lion flinched and moved backwards. She sought higher ground and looked back at us. By then she must have been trying to figure out what the hell kind of creature she was dealing with that had suddenly became taller and wider than it had been a moment before. Or maybe she just thought we were too crazy to bother with. We kept on making threatening gestures.

Luckily, she made the decision to run off.

Slowly, I lowered Katrina to the ground. My heart was thudding hard against my ribcage, and I didn't want her to hear it. I felt almost high with adrenaline as we watched the lion trot away, after a few backward glances.

I brought my gaze back to her. "You ok?"

She looked up at me. Her lovely eyes enormous and her eyelashes wet. She must have been crying.

"Um, yeah … I'm fine. That was unbelievable," she replied gruffly.

I didn't answer, but still held onto her waist keeping her close. What was it about this woman? I couldn't leave her alone for a minute without her getting herself into another spot of bother.

She shivered. "She could have killed us both. I thought she was going to eat me before you came along."

I smiled. "Well, she didn't. I got to you first." Jesus, I almost finished that sentence with the words. *And so I get to eat you.*

"Yeah. You did." She twisted in my arms to look back where the lion had disappeared to. "What made you come down here?"

I didn't want to tell her the effect she had on me. With all the other women in my life, I could let them walk away. No matter if they were crying or hurt. I just didn't care. With her, I find it impossible. It hurts me to see her hurt. "Come on, let's get out of here before we meet any of the other unfriendly locals."

My grip was still firm around her from adrenaline and fear. I loosened it to let her move freely away from me. She didn't. She held my shoulders and looked searchingly into my eyes. "OK, let's go." She made to take a step and winced in pain.

Instinctively, I caught her. "What have you done to yourself?"

"Argh! It's my knee. I must have banged it up pretty bad."

I frowned. "How?"

"When I fell."

I shook my head in exasperation. "You fell too? Seriously, you are a risk to yourself."

"Until I met you I was a strong independent woman." A wary note had crept into her voice.

"Maybe you're just not mountain woman material," I said, not wanting to argue again. I didn't want to start caring about what happened to her. She was nothing to me. As soon as the snow melted she'd be gone back to the city. I just needed to keep it light.

"Aw, the mountain will get used to me after a while, and then she'll love me. Everybody does."

Yeah, I bet they did. Grumpily, I put my arm around her waist so I could act as her crutch. "Here, lean your weight on me."

She hobbled along on one leg, most of her weight supported on me. It was slow going up the mountain, but it actually felt nice being close to Katrina, our bodies working together in perfect synchronization. Whenever there was something in our path and we were out of step, she felt the pain and gritted her teeth. It was a lot like our every exchange since I heard her car crash over the pass. Every time we get out of step with each other, she feels the pain of my harshness.

I felt sorry for being an asshole to her back in the workshop. I didn't know how to react to her seeing the sculpture. Of course, it was a sculpture of her, but I didn't think my artistic skills were good enough for her to recognize herself in my piece. Maybe I do have some abilities. I was so shocked that she saw herself reflected that I lashed out, I hurt her out of my own embarrassment. I didn't want her to know she'd gotten to me right from the moment I pulled her out of the car.

"You know ..." I just couldn't find the words to explain what happened in the workshop. To tell her how I felt is the kind of language that I don't have. I didn't think I ever would. But I could be decent. "I'm sorry. About earlier. Haven't ever shown anybody my sculpture work before. It was too soon."

"I'm sorry too, for snooping around. Next time, I'll just knock, huh?"

She smiled, and something deep in my stomach sparked and rippled electricity all through me. How another person can create that chemical reaction in someone else is marvelous, just from a smile.

"Do you need to rest for a minute before we carry on?"

"No, I can keep going. Let's just get back to the cabin, and then maybe you can make me another one of those drinks you've secretly got stashed around."

Ahead I saw a rock and I knew I didn't want to see her face crunch up with pain. I swept her into my arms and hoisted her over my shoulder. She squealed with surprise then began to laugh, that rocky, sexy, confident laugh that I loved. The sound was beautiful in the desolate scenery. When she was gone I would remember her laugh on these mountains. It occurred to me that her presence had changed the mountains for me. It won't be the same. What I had appreciated as my solitude would feel empty.

"I'm too heavy for you to carry me all the way," she protested.

I could feel the delectable warmth from her hip against my cheek. God, I was obsessed with this woman. "You're not heavy. We'll have to have a look at your knee when we get back."

"Have you got any other forms of pain relief around that you've been keeping under wraps?"

"Well, I can think of one thing that might help," I murmured.

She laughed again. "Hang on, did you just flirt with me? Was that what that was? Well, I am astounded!"

That made me laugh.

"Oh, my God, and now he's laughing. Are you the same person? Do you have an evil twin, and you're like the good guy of the duo? Have I been with the bad Cade and now the good twin has arrived?"

"Hey, come on, that's not totally fair. The bad Cade did rescue you from your crashed car. I was nice ... some, right?"

It was fun to laugh with her.

"And that's not what I meant by the way. Well, it kind of was, but what I actually meant was some ice-cold water for your knee. A dip in the creek may do you a world of good. It will certainly bring any swelling you have down. I use the creek every morning for that very thing."

"You don't!" She laughed so loudly, she was in danger of setting off another avalanche. "I can't believe you just said that! You actually go into the creek every morning to get your *swelling* to go down? That is hilarious. You know, there are other ways of doing that."

"Are you flirting with me?"

"Maybe. I haven't decided if you're worth the hassle yet. You're kind of hard to read, you know?"

"Yeah. I guess I am."

"Why is that? Why are you so complicated?"

"I don't think I am."

"What's up? Why have you turned all serious on me? It's like a dark cloud just rolled over you."

"Nothing's up. I'm just not complicated. You're reading too much into me."

"OK."

She must have thought the evil twin Cade was surfacing because she stopped talking. She switched the fun off, didn't ask any more questions. She just lay quietly on my shoulder and I focused on getting us up the mountain without exacerbating the pain in her knee. Maybe she was right to back away from me.

CADE

Back at the cabin I eased her down onto the stool. "Are you alright?"

"Yeah. I think I'm just kind of exhausted from it all. The adrenaline and endorphins are gone. That experience with the mountain lion, that was intense. I'm starting to feel the effects of everything now."

I took a step back and ran my hands through my hair awkwardly. She was right, the adrenaline high was gone and we were back where we started. "Ok. Let's get you something for the pain."

"How about an Irish coffee? I was drinking coffee when I set out this morning looking for you. You could put it back on the stove and then put a shot of whiskey in there. That would help my knee."

I lit the stove to get some heat under the coffee. While we waited for the stove to get hot, I made a pallet on the floor for her, collecting up all the cushions and quilts I had around the cabin.

"Can I ask you something?"

"Is it personal?"

"I don't think so."

"Go on then."

"When I was in your workroom I saw no other sculptures. Where is all your other work? Do you sell them in town or something?"

"I don't sell my work," I said shortly.

"Oh, what do you do with them then?"

I didn't turn around to face her. "I break it up and use for firewood."

"What? Why?"

I didn't reply and for a while there was only silence.

"Why don't you sell it?"

"You sell something if you need the money. I don't."

"But why would you not want to keep them?"

"You keep something if you value it. I don't value these pieces of wood."

"But the sculpture you are working on right now is so beautiful. It's odd to spend so much time on something and then to destroy it."

"Everything in this world is destined to decay and turn to dust eventually, Katrina."

"Yes, but how can you bear to destroy something you have put so much love and attention on?"

In my mind's eyes, I saw the jagged metal crush and tear the flesh I had created and loved. The image so vivid I wanted to gag. I turned to face her. "You should elevate your knee. Lay down here and then put your knee up on the stool."

"Ok."

I think she expected me to help her down to the floor with an arm around her waist and supporting her weight. Instead, I slipped an arm around her waist and under her knees and scooped her up in my arms again.

Then I floated her down to the floor wanting to make the moment last. As I released her, I felt her body relax into the floor as though she would have welcomed me to join her. Instinct led me to create these moments of closeness, but something inside stopped me from continuing to the next step. Truth was: she terrified me.

The coffee percolated bubbling coffee over the stovetop.

"One medicinal coffee coming up," I said, moving away from her.

"Are you going to have one too? I don't want to drink alone."

"Yeah. I'll have one with you."

I found a spare chipped cup from the cupboard and filled that with coffee, then added a shot of whiskey to each, and handed the good cup to her.

"Thanks."

I felt awkward and I didn't know where to put myself so I switched on the radio to pick up an update on the weather.

"You know, I did catch a trout this morning for us."

"You did? Well, I'm absolutely starving, so I guess I'll have to give it a try."

"I'll cook it outside otherwise we're going to have to smell trout for the next few days. If you're hungry I'll put it on the fire now."

"Well, you can have your coffee first."

"No, it's ok. I'll have it outside. I better get that fire going anyway."

I needed a reason to be away from her. My appetite for her was growing, as was my fear of how strongly I felt about her. Just before I hit the door, the radio broadcast caught my ear.

"Good morning, Rocky Mountains! We're just coming up to the noon hour in just a few minutes here, and we've got great news from the National Weather Service for you now. That recent winter storm that brought heavy snowfall to the valleys and central mountains is expected to move on in the next 24 hours. The storm has caused severe disruption to the roads, and has resulted in school closures across several counties. Now, we all know if a Colorado school closes, then it's pretty bad out there, right?

Also, the Colorado Department of Transport says roads will begin to be cleared over the next 24 hours as that fog hanging over us begins to dissipate. The heavy mist has thus far prevented road crews from being able to safely get out there and clear away not only the heavy snowfall that dumped on us over the last few days, but also the road closures caused by the avalanche over Dogwood Pass. It's been a mess out there people, but the end is in sight and it looks like at long last spring is just around the corner!"

"So ... looks like I'll be able to get out of your hair soon."

"Yeah. Sounds like it." I kept my voice light.

"Maybe even by tomorrow, huh?"

"Well, we need to give them a chance to get it all cleared. It's not going to happen as quickly as they say."

"Oh, ok. So, I guess we just listen out for the reports to know when we'd be able to get down to town?"

"Um, yeah. So, maybe tomorrow, or the next day."

"We should do something special tonight. Maybe I'll raid your freezer again and cook us up something tasty. Would you be up for that? I mean, as long as I wouldn't be stepping on your toes by cooking."

I thought about it and I didn't like the idea of her gone.

"We don't have to do it. It was just an idea," she added quickly, biting her lip uncertainly.

"No, that sounds good. But you should wait to make that raid until after you've tried the trout. You might love it so much, you'll be sending me back down to the creek to catch more." I smiled at her. "It could happen."

I went out to the fire pit before I messed up another perfectly good exchange between us by turning into an asshole again. The news forecast was supposed to be good news, but it wasn't to me. I should have got rid of her that second morning. Letting her stay these extra days was a mistake, because she sunk into my life. I wanted her, wanted her around, and not having her around would hurt. I couldn't imagine her going now. It was funny what you got used to after even only a short period of time. I've got used to having this infuriating, sexy, intelligent, beautiful woman around.

Scraps from my old finished sculpture formed the base of the fire. I loved building a fire. It was one of the simple pleasures of life.

"Hey, I thought you might need these." Katrina came out of the cabin hobbling and carrying tin foil and a seasoning shaker.

"Thanks." I took the items from her and felt a pulse of electricity when our fingers touched. "You should keep off that knee."

She grinned widely. "After the amount of whiskey you put in my coffee it's starting to feel a lot better. The swelling is starting to go down a little."

She eased herself down onto a log next to the fire with all of her weight expertly balanced on one leg.

"Impressive," I commented.

Her eyes sparkled. "Yeah, I've got dancer's balance."

Silence fell between us as I once again killed the conversation. It wasn't that I didn't know how to talk to people. I get that there are lines that people throw in chatting that they want you to follow so that they can tell you things about themselves. I understand that was how it worked. I just didn't like it. I didn't want to be fished at for conversation. I also liked silence. My guess was Katrina didn't though. I put her out of her misery.

"You sure you want to see this? I'm about to clean the fish. Its guts are going to be pulled out. If you want you can go inside and I'll call you back out when it's over."

"It's alright. I'm tough."

I hid a smile. "You do seem kind of strong, but I wouldn't go so far as tough."

"Oh yeah? And where did you, Mr. Tough Guy, learn to clean a fish? YouTube videos?" She laughed in her teasing way. "You are an absolute poser of a mountain man. I come from a lot rougher stuff than you ever did."

"I'm here now."

"Yes, you are."

Katrina let the silence fall between us this time. After a while she said, "Well, how did you get out here? What was your life like before?"

"I uh ..." I stoked the fire with a stick and searched for what I could possibly say that wouldn't make her run screaming away from me. Images, memories flashed across my mind, but all of them terrible. Nothing I could ever tell a girl like her.

"Tell you what, you just concentrate on getting that awful-smelling fish cleaned that's still got his eyeballs on me, and I'll tell you about me. The me up until I crashed my car in the trees."

She sounded enthusiastic, like she wanted to tell me her life story. I couldn't imagine anything worse than having to reciprocate that experience.

"No! You don't have to do that," I said.

She seemed shocked and confused by my outburst.

"It's alright. I want to."

"Yes, but I don't. I don't want to talk. About anything, me, or the past, or how you got to where you were running from some guy over Dogwood Pass—"

"I told you, I hardly knew him."

"I know, you said that. Listen, I don't want to sound nasty again, because I know I've been mean since you've arrived, but surely you can use your common sense here and understand that I want to distance myself from what I was before I came to this mountain. Otherwise I wouldn't be out here. So I don't want to hear about your life because I can't reciprocate. Not right now anyway."

I poked around in the fire again. Katrina watched the flickers float upwards and I wanted to stare at the beautiful expression on her face. I forced myself to turn away. "All I can give you is trout right now."

Her gaze skittered over to me and she smiled, like an innocent child. Just happy for that moment. I was relieved to have not ruined another moment with my intentionally awkward social skills.

"Fine. I'll take that. But you're going to have to put a serious amount of seasoning on that bad boy because the last trout I ate tasted like creek water."

I threw my head back and laughed. Oh, Katrina. Did the mountain really give you to me?

KATRINA

"Ok, so you made it taste like ... fish."

Cade laughed again, which was absolutely gorgeous. He looked even sexier when he was relaxed and enjoying himself. He took the tin foil parcel from my lap and emptied the remaining contents into the fire. My heart tingled as his hand brushed against my thigh.

"Can't leave food leftovers out here. Bears will be on it tonight rustling up everything. I learned that the hard way."

"Seems like you got a lot of furry friends around here. You ever run into anyone on two legs?"

"Not really. There's Beau higher up the mountain, but generally it's just me and the wild ones unless I go into town."

"That must have been hard to get used to, living in the midst of wild, dangerous animals?"

"It's not any more dangerous than living around humans." His mouth twisted. "In fact, it's probably safer out here."

"So … town. Guess we'll be going into town tomorrow. See about getting my hunk of junk towed off the mountain."

Cade looked at me a moment, then out towards the creek. He bounced his knee, which I've never noticed him do before. He was thinking about something.

"Before we go anywhere, let's see if we can get your knee fixed up."

"How? I mean I know exactly what's happened to it. I've twisted it like this before at work and it'll heal by itself in time."

"Let's go to the creek."

"What? I'm not going in the freezing cold water!"

"Yeah. I think you are." He beamed his white, straight teeth at me.

This man was quite the enigma. He took freezing baths in the creek while there was a hot spring, lived in a messy cabin, ate tin food, and yet took exquisite care of himself physically. He looked so good and tasty; I was totally prepared to go marching in that icy water if he said to. He stood up and crossed to my side of the fire, putting himself directly in front of me. He smiled down at me, an evil smile.

"What are you doing?" I asked nervously.

Before I knew what was happening, he scooped me up from my tree stump seat and carried me towards the creek.

"Argh! Put me down. Cade, please put me down," I screamed, but he just laughed and a sense of fun started to pour into every cell in my body. I clung to him as he jogged with me in his arms, his feet thudding in the snow.

He got right to the edge of the water and pretended he was going to throw me in. Instantly, I fought against being tossed and gripped onto his broad back. I pressed myself against him completely. We were so close I could hear his heart and it was beating fast.

Our laughter subsided suddenly and we were left standing in the snow, our bodies stuck to each other. The quiet trickling water beside us made for a beautiful moment. I looked into the gold specks in his eyes, then let my gaze deliberately slip down to his sensuous mouth. I couldn't make it clearer that I wanted him to kiss me.

He swallowed hard. "Let's get your knee fixed. Hold onto me and I'll lower you in the water."

I didn't let my disappointment show. "What about my jeans?"

"They're going to get wet ... unless you take them off?"

I played along. "Hmm. That's your idea, huh? Bring me out here in this freezing water, and get me to take my clothes off?"

"Trust me. You'll feel better for it. Come on, at least, take your boots and socks off."

"Don't worry, I'm not shy. I'll take my jeans off. Besides, who wants to walk back to the cabin wearing freezing wet jeans? Unless you were planning on carrying me back too? Well, I better not count on that, I never know how long our moments of being friends will last before I piss you off again."

He put me on the ground, and kneeling down in front of me pulled my boots off while I held onto the thick cords of muscles in his shoulders.

"You might want to keep away from the socks. They could stink," I joked.

He pulled the first off and looking up at me brought it to his nose and inhaled. For a moment I was frozen by that purely animalistic, completely primal action. I saw his eyes darken, then he put his head down and removed my other sock. He stood and took a step away from me. I swallowed hard. The air around us had changed. It was throbbing with our awareness of each other.

I whipped my jeans down to my ankles. Stepping out of them, I picked them up and draped them over his shoulder. The more intimate parts of me were still concealed by my big coat, but my legs were bare. He looked down at them.

"Well, that's a sight for sore eyes."

I laughed at his response. "Oh, God, I can't believe it. That's the first compliment you've ever given me. I tell you what, I'm going to hold out for a better one before I start counting them."

He looked at me hungrily, and if I had been with any other man I would have known that a kiss was on its way, but I'd been burned too many times by him and I wasn't going there unless he led me there by the hand.

I hugged myself. "So, what am I supposed to do, just stand out here in the freezing cold and hope that my swollen knee goes down? Or am I supposed to drop myself in this water, oh wise, mountain man?"

"Um, yeah, wade out to the middle so you can get your knee under the water."

"You're kidding me? No, cowboy, that's not how this is going to work. If I'm going in, then you're coming in with me. Boots and socks off! Let's go!"

He smiled and turned his chin down flirtatiously.

"Alright then. You asked for it."

KATRINA

He kicked off his snow boots, pulled off his socks and then stood opposite me. He was a lot taller than me. He looked in my eyes and grinned. Then he whipped me up in his arms again and tore off into the water still wearing his jeans.

"Wait! No fair!"

Cade carried me out to where the water was thigh deep on him. He dipped down in the water crouched on his knees and held me across his lap to force my knee into the icy water.

The feeling was so intense I lost control of myself momentarily and screamed at the shock of how cold it was.

He just laughed and said, "Relax. Give it a minute and you'll be fine. And your knee will be as good as new."

"Argh! It's so cold! Argh. I can't take it, anymore. Let me up. Cade, let me up. Come on. It's not funny anymore."

But he kept a tight hold around my waist, both of us submerged to the waist in the freezing water. "You've got it. Just hang in there. You can do it."

"I can't! Let me go!" I screamed.

"Just one more minute. One minute and we'll get out and get back to the fire. Just think about the fire. The warm blankets I'm going to wrap you in. And the hot drink of whiskey coffee that's going to be warming you from the inside."

Cade talking to me, encouraging me to accomplish something as simple as being braver than the cold caught me. I stopped screaming. My breath was frantic.

"Deep breaths. You can do this."

After a couple of inhales, I began to slow down the pace of my breathing. I looked ahead at the creek ambling over rocks at the bank, the mountains in the distance and then to the beautiful, strong man holding me tight and telling me that I can do something difficult. He was trying to help me. I stopped fighting. And felt humbled by him, by my situation. He was a good person. I might have fallen in love with him at that moment.

"Good job. Well done. You've got another thirty seconds and then we're out of here. I promise you, your knee will be a lot better. You've almost done this. Almost there, well done." His voice was soothing, almost hypnotic. The freezing water swirled around us as I stared up into his eyes.

"Ok," I whispered.

The truth was I was completely flustered by what Cade had just done for me. It may seem silly to anyone else, but it was one of the nicest things any man had ever done for me.

Maybe I hadn't been lucky in love before, but he seemed to genuinely care for me. He disregarded how cold he must have been himself to help me. His arm, the one that had been tightly wrapped around me, came up to gently trace my jaw.

I wanted him to kiss me. I needed to feel those full sensuous lips on mine, and after that much more; much, much more. I just needed him to kiss me first. I had to know that it came from him too. He has to be the instigator for this to work. In my head I was screaming for him to make the move. Do it! Please, do it.

"Time's up. We've got to get out of this freezing water now."

"Uh huh."

I couldn't believe I wanted to stay in the freezing water. Literally one minute earlier I was screaming to come out, but I would have given anything to stay put long enough to have a luscious kiss with this oddly gruff, strong, honest, caring, mysterious man.

He carried me to the bank and stepped into his own boots. He dropped down to a knee to pick up my socks and boots.

"Here, you carry these. I'll carry you."

With only the sound of snow crunching beneath his footsteps, his breathing becoming heavier. We didn't speak, but it didn't feel like silence between us. Our heads were filled with the ideas of what might happen next. At least, mine was. Maybe he was just thinking about being alone again, running off to his workshop to avoid me. I hoped he was thinking about us. I kept my arms around his neck and prayed he wouldn't be able to find a way out of them.

The light was beginning to fade behind the mountain as we

arrived back at the cabin. It left a pink glow over everything. I couldn't have asked for a more romantic setting. Cade set me down onto the pallet of blankets and cushions on the floor. I didn't ask for it because I refused to instigate this encounter. I'd never believe it was a genuine desire from him if I started it, but I swear, I gave him my most soft, green light, come and get it eyes I had.

"I've got to get the fire going to warm you up now," he said, but he stayed kneeling down next to me on the floor.

I licked my lips and watched his gaze slide down to my mouth. "What about you? Don't you need to come out of those wet jeans?"

He blinked. "Um hm. I need to do that. I ... um ... should take them off. That OK with you?"

We were talking about wet clothes, but we were *not* talking about wet clothes. We held each other's gaze and made a secret, unspoken agreement that we were going to have sex. A buzzing sensation ran all over my body. I felt like I needed to do a huge, comedy gulp at the prospect of this beautifully sculpted man, who hadn't been with a woman in a significant amount of time, ravishing me. At the mere thought of us touching made my body prepare itself for his entry. I felt myself become wet with desire for him.

Cade rose to stoke the fire on the wood-burning stove. He placed our boots nearby to dry them, and hung our socks on the line above. His movements were deliberate. As if he was doing it to test himself. All he really wanted to do was fall on me and take me hard.

I took off my sweater that was soggy around the bottom and

sat there just in a t-shirt and wet panties. My knee was much better, or maybe it was just the feeling of anticipation raging through me over Cade.

He stood in the middle of the room. "Shall I make us a hot drink? To warm you up from the inside?"

I debated taking the bait on that one. I'd love nothing more than for him to warm me up from the inside.

"Yes, that's sounds nice." What the hell was wrong with me? The last thing in the world I wanted was a drink. And I think I could safely say the same for him. But something had happened to me. I'd suddenly turned shy. What I really wanted was to start this thing off so we could get over this awkwardness and here I was playing the coy maiden. Cade fumbled around in the kitchen area. After a few moments, I smelled something wonderful like vanilla and cinnamon.

"Wow, that smells delicious. Is that our drinks that smell so good?" I twisted around to look at Cade in the kitchen area.

"Um, no, I just lit a candle."

"Oh."

I saw him peel down his wet jeans and hang them over the line. His legs were long, lean and sculpted. He seemed distracted. "Do you mind if we wait on the hot drink?"

"No, that's ok ..."

Before I could finish speaking Cade crossed the room, took my face in his strong hands, and kissed me. It was like plugging my finger into a live socket. My whole body felt electrified. We were two pieces that were meant to fit together and we had denied ourselves for so long our coming together was violent. Our lips fell into each other's and we devoured each other. We were like animals. Hungry, crazed. His lips felt more perfect over mine than I'd even imagined. Something feral, ancient, and stronger than lust filled my body.

KATRINA

https://www.youtube.com/watch?v=mQZmCJUSC6g

He pushed me back down to the floor as the kiss became more savage. I clawed desperately at his shirt, he pulled at mine, then snatched away from our kiss long enough to yank the damn thing over my head.

He looked at my breasts beneath my lace bra. The look in his eyes was so intense and heated I felt as if I had never been looked at before by a man. He splayed his large hands around the weight of my breast and groaned. Running his index finger along the inside of the lace he brushed it against my nipple. It shot through me like a bolt of electricity. I reared back at the jolt.

Our eyes locked and his were so dark and mysterious with desire, my stomach lurched. Transfixed, I watched a myriad of emotions roll across his face. Yes, I had caught glimpses of lust in his eyes before, but he hadn't looked at me like this.

With such burning need. As if he had been denied too long. As if he wanted to devour me.

All our time together had consisted of him building a wall between us, and yet, at that moment, I felt as if I'd known him forever. As if I had always belonged to him, body and soul. There was no one else but him.

"Do you have any idea what you've been doing to me these last days?" he asked hoarsely.

Exhilaration tore through me. "Show me."

He pulled the lace down so that the tip of my nipple sat above it. He growled with lust at the sight. His face was a blur as his mouth swooped down. I nearly screamed when it latched on to my flesh and he immediately began to suck, hard. His other hand reached down to my panties, as I lost my last grip on sanity. My hips bucked when his tongue flicked at my nub.

Crouched over me he began to undress quickly. I watched with widened eyes.

Naked, he was the most glorious combination of bulging sinew, strength, manly angles, and beautiful blue tattoos. Awestruck, I ran my hands down his wide chest, his rock hard stomach, then moved lower to grip his thick erection in my hands. Still on his knees, he dropped his head backwards and arched his back as he relished the feeling.

"Oh, fuck," he groaned. "You're so sexy. You're driving me wild." He pulled himself out of my grasp and curled in on himself, almost to a ball, to slow down his physical responses. When he unfolded his frame, he pushed me back down to the floor. He kissed my neck and ran his hand to the back of my hair.

Cade licked and kissed his way down my neck, along my clavicle and to my breasts. I have large breasts for my small frame, a fact that I hated while I was at school. He sucked on one nipple and ran his thumb around the other.

I arched my back to let him know I liked it and pushed my pelvis into him. He was listening intently to my physical cues because his tongue picked up the motion of his thumb over my nipple and his other hand slipped down my stomach into my panties. It only took him a second to find the exact spot he needed to be.

Ahhhh! I ached with pleasure. I pulled my knees up and widened my legs. I wanted more. I was out of my mind, on the verge of ecstasy.

"Wait …" he panted. "We don't have … do you have anything?"

"No," I said. "I mean, I do in my car. Don't you have anything?"

"Hell no. I live alone on a mountain. I never expected to be in this position."

We looked at each other. His eyes were glazed, desire poured out of every pore on the man's body. In the quiet of the cabin, his heart was as loud as a drum.

"Fuck," he swore.

"I'm not one to be risky with my body. I only see one option here."

"I see sixty-nine of them."

I would have laughed out loud, but my body was on the precipice of orgasm.

"Ladies first," he said, roughly grabbing my legs.

I squealed as he opened my thighs wide. Without any kind of warning he placed his hot mouth between my legs and sucked my whole pussy into his mouth. In the history of quick orgasms, none could possibly equal mine.

Grabbing his head, I climaxed.

Just like that.

Gushing into his mouth, screaming his name, and thrashing my limbs, while he held my clit captive and growled with satisfaction for having so effortlessly made me soar free. It was amazing, and I was still whimpering when it was over. The delicious sensation of his beard against my inner thighs and his lapping tongue made me determined to make him scream my name too.

"Your turn," I announced, lifting my head up, even though I still felt almost dizzy after such a hard climax.

KATRINA

He lifted his head. "I'm not finished yet."

His voice was dark, deep, rough, and sexy. It made my hair stand on end. Everything that had happened was like sensory overload. "I need a break, baby. Let me do you first, okay?"

He stared at me for a moment longer before rolling over. I was shocked to see how big he was. The urge to impale myself on that massive shaft, all the way to the hilt, condom be damned, was nearly overpowering, but I got on my hands and knees and began to crawl over to him. As my breasts neared his mouth though, he captured a nipple in it while his hand kneaded the other breast. All over again, I felt myself get wet and swollen for him, if that was even possible. I wanted to tell him to stop it, but what he was doing was far too distracting and delectable for me to even think of stopping him. His hand found my pussy and I felt him insert one thick, rough finger into me while his thumb played with my clit.

Oh, Sweet Jesus.

I couldn't move. I couldn't think. I just stayed in that position until I went over the edge. The orgasm was so intense I collapsed in a heap, half my body on Cade, and the other half on the floor. I imagined my scream leaving the cabin and travelling over the snow-capped mountain.

He stroked my hair. "Now it's your turn."

I could smell him from where he lay, cum leaking from his erect cock. His scent was driving me crazy, sweet yet raw and totally masculine. I shuffled forward and slid my tongue along his warm shaft. His taste matched his scent. Utterly seductive.

I sucked him further into my mouth, my lips gliding over the satin smoothness, until his cock bumped the back of my throat. When I eased up a little to keep from gagging, I felt him pull his hips away. Immediately, I drove back down. I loved the taste of him and the sensation of his hardness throbbing in my mouth, and I wasn't letting him go anywhere.

He was all mine. Every last inch.

I cupped his balls in my hand while rolling and stroking them. Inhaling through my nose I sank all the way down. Further than before. His eyes widened as his cock slipped into my throat.

"Christ, Katrina, I'm not going to be able to hold on much longer."

High on how little control he seemed to have left, I drove down until his entire cock was buried in my throat. I was aching for it to be inside me, but I ignored the craving, and focused solely on his pleasure. My tongue was flat and caressing.

"Oh, fuck, I'm coming," he growled. His fingers clawed into my hair and he tried to pull me off him as his hips began to buck uncontrollably.

I grabbed his hips and held on.

His abs were clenched and a sheen of sweat glistened on his skin. "You want me to come in your mouth?"

Looking deep into his eyes, I nodded.

He lost control then. Rearing he began to fuck my mouth harder. I let him thrust into my mouth and throat while I watched his face. He was savoring every second of this. A roar from somewhere deep inside of him tore out of his throat as his plunges became faster and more urgent.

Still I sucked. Up and down the long thick length of him. My cheeks were hollow and my jaw had begun to ache. His movements became more forceful, like a piston. I felt his cock become thicker in my mouth, the veins bulging against my tongue, as the first spurt of salty cum hit the back of my throat.

Grabbing my face, he drove the rest of his climax into my throat. I never took my eyes off him. I felt his hot seed slide down my throat and fill my belly. Eventually, his thrusts slowed, then stilled.

While his breathing returned to normal, I licked his cock clean. Then I looked up at him and grinned. "Well, we could go through the rest of those sixty-nine options, and hike down to my car for supplies at first light?"

He scratched his chin and looked out of the window. It was already pitch black. "That's a plan, I suppose."

"We'll fill up on appetizers and wait for the main course." I sighed, resigned to the prospect of waiting. I refused to make silly mistakes with my body. I had no room for babies or diseases in my life. There was still plenty of fun to be had without intercourse.

"In the meantime, I have an idea," I added.

"By the look in your eyes I bet I'm going to like it."

"Here, sit on the stool. I'll do a dance for you. It's kind of a specialty of mine."

"Oh, my God."

"Have you got any music?"

"Only what's on the radio."

I scanned along the airwaves to find anything I could move to. The channel that came through strongest played classical music. It was not exactly sexy, but then I found a country channel that was playing Carly Simon's *You're So Vain*. Perfect. I could work with that.

There were a couple of beams in the middle of the cabin. I could use those like a pole to show my strength and flexibility; and to make him drool. All my clothes except my panties were already off, so no strip tease segments to this dance.

I started off with my back to him on the other side of the beam. Turning my uninjured knee out I traced my foot up my calf and then pointed it out to the side. Taking hold of the beam with my opposite arm, I hooked my outstretched heel in my other hand. Raising my leg out to the side I levered myself into something that looked like a standing split.

"Oh, my God," Cade ejaculated.

I held onto the beam and lowered myself so that my ass perched out from behind the beam in full view. With his attention fully captured, I danced around him, as sensuous as a snake in the garden of Eden. I moved my hips so close to his face, I actually caught him helplessly inhaling my scent. As his hand came up to grab me I slipped away.

I was letting the music guide my pace, but I was also listening out for cues from Cade. I wanted to give him so much visually I'd have him not just hungry but mercilessly hooked and addicted before we even began our next session.

I centered myself against the beam once more, let go of my outstretched leg and let it wrap around the beam behind me. Keeping my foot tucked there for balance, I leaned the top half of my body down and allowed my breasts to fall forward. Then, I twisted my body to a sideways position with my leg still hooked up to expose a sly view of my lady glory.

"Lord, have mercy."

I giggled at his response, but kept it going: there was still the piece-de-résistance. Gracefully, I plucked out a long scarf hanging from a nearby hook and threw it around one of the beams. Facing Cade now, I held on to the two ends of the scarf and began to lean back as I slowly drew myself up. Hanging from the beam I suddenly opened my legs while keeping them straight.

There.

He was getting the full-frontal treatment. My whole pussy was at eye level, open, and exposed to his gaze. I knew I was wet and I was showing him just how wet I was.

"Oh God, I can't take it, anymore." Cade jumped up.

I turned around and shimmied my ass at him.

In a flash, he pulled on a pair of jeans and his shirt. Without a word, he snatched a torch from a shelf and bolted out of the door, grabbing his boots on the way.

I burst out laughing.

CADE

I burst through the door with all the luggage I found in her car. She didn't just have one bag; there was an overnight bag, a purse, and a brown sack of groceries.

"You brought everything?"

"Yeah, I didn't know which one had the condoms in it so I brought them all."

She laughed at me.

"I'm glad you find it funny because I just ran down the mountains in the pitch dark, half-naked, and with a massive hard-on so I didn't fancy doing that twice."

She rolled on the floor with only her hair draped around her, laughing, absolutely naked, and breathtakingly beautiful.

I felt something flick inside me like a pilot light coming back on. It was a feeling that hadn't been there for so long it actually took me a minute to remember exactly what it was. Joy.

I dropped the bags on the floor beside her. "Go on, find the damn condoms. I want to pick up where we left off before my insane sprint down the mountains."

While she sat up and unzipped one of her bags, I rubbed my frozen hands together over the stove to warm them up before I touched her warm skin. She found a packet and, eyes shining, held it up triumphantly.

"Now show me your cunt again," I ordered. "Exactly how you showed me just now."

She shivered with excitement. Her eyes were glazed over as she lay back, spread her thighs wide, and showed me her sweet pussy. The flesh was pink and wet. Dripping wet. Fuck, just watching it made my mouth water for another taste of it. My dick was hard and ready to fuck. There was something between us and it was intense. I was swollen to the point of pain as I flung my clothes off and crouched between her legs. She was so fucking beautiful she looked unreal on the floor of my cabin.

I fitted the rubber around my shaft, and put a hand on her stomach. Seeing my callused, rough hands on her fine skin sent a jolt of excitement directly to my cock. I never wanted to *claim* a woman before. Plant a flag and say, I own this goddamn territory. But she made me want to act in that primitive way.

This woman made the breath hitch in my throat.

The scent of her pretty pussy filled my nostrils and maddened my blood. I pushed two fingers into her tight entrance and she made a lusty sound between a sob and a moan. Her body arched, lifting those full breasts up and exposing the creamy curve of her throat. It sent me into liquid meltdown.

"You finally get your wish. Wrap your legs around my hips, baby."

Her lips were parted and her breath was coming out in shallow gasps. I swear, I'd never seen anything sexier than her at that moment.

I let the head of my cock press against her wet entrance.

"God, Cade," she choked.

Slowly, I penetrated her, my cock head squelching against her juices, as it slid past the entrance.

"Oh, my God," she gasped when she was impaled to the hilt on my dick. I paused and let her body adjust to my length and thickness. She lifted her head and her mouth found my lips. The kiss was hot and wet, our breathing mingled. I pulled out and plunged forward again, burying myself all the way in. I ate her cry of shock and ecstasy. She buried her face in the crook of my neck and nipped at my skin with her small teeth. That just made me swear and pound even deeper into her. I fucked her like I was never going to stop. She fisted her fingers in my hair and stifled her moans against my neck. With each hard thrust her clit was being pounded and she was being reduced to a quivering mess. It felt amazing. She was wide open and taking every inch of me.

"Oh God," she gasped brokenly against my neck.

While I pounded her, I yanked her head up by her hair and captured her mouth in a fierce kiss. I mimicked the thrusting of my cock with my tongue in her mouth while she sucked blindly. I could feel her orgasm bubbling up through her body. Her pussy started clenching my driving cock. It was pure bliss. I kept on banging against her swollen clit until she gave a frantic wail.

"Oh God. Oh. Oh. Oh," she screamed as her mind blanked and every inch of her body tightened as her climax raced through her. Her pussy was like a tight fist around my cock and it was driving me out of my mind. I started to pulse. I thrust hard one last time, then my balls draw up, and I started offloading. I kept thrusting into her, letting her squeezing muscles milk every last drop of seed out of me. Even when I finished shooting I continued riding out the orgasm. Her body was quivering.

"That was amazing," she whispered, her eyes dark and glazed.

I didn't dare speak.

We clung to each other. Like survivors of something incredible, unbelievable, unexpected.

CADE

I woke up suddenly. A weird dream where my mother was sitting at the end of my bed and combing her hair. I frowned. Strange, because I hadn't seen my mother in two years and had hardly ever thought of her during that time.

Katrina's warm, smooth body was next to me.

I turned to look at her. Blue dawn light poured in through the little square window next to me. It turned her gold hair into silver. Without touching her I ran my nose along the length of her neck, inhaling her scent. She still smelt of sex and excitement.

Not wanting to wake her up, I watched her sleep.

Now, I knew why I'd fought so hard to keep her at a distance. Some part of me always recognized I'd never be able to stop once I started anything. As I had guessed I was already lost to her smell, taste, and body.

I crept an arm around her, and she reciprocated by twisting her legs with mine.

"Morning," she mumbled, still half asleep. I watched her try to open her eyes, but it must have been too much trouble, because she made a sleepy sound, and simply rolled to her side. With her back to me she wriggled her naked ass into my erection and calmly went back to sleep.

A few incredible seconds passed while I stared at her golden head in surprise. Then she froze and twisted back, her eyes still slumberous, but sexy, oh so sexy. "Oh, you're real. I thought I was still dreaming."

I had to smile. That was the cutest reaction I'd ever had to morning wood. She looked at me shyly.

"Have you been fantasizing about me, baby?"

Her cheeks looked like they were on fire. "Maybe," she mumbled and turning over buried her blush in the pillows.

My curiosity stirred. I rolled her on her back, threw a leg over her, and supported by my forearms hovered over her body. "Oh yeah? Tell me what you fantasized about?"

"Oh, I have a few scenarios," she said not quite meeting my eyes.

Images flashed through my mind, sizzling, intriguing images that made my cock jerk and hurt. I kissed a rosy nipple. "Tell me."

She licked her lips. "It's not all that exciting. Just a run of the mill mountain man fantasy."

I grinned. There was no way she was leaving this bed without telling me. "What is a run of the mill mountain man fantasy?"

"You know, the usual wood chopping, bearded man stuff. Nothing special."

"So tell me what it was. I want to know what turns you on."

"I'd really like to keep that private if you don't mind," she mumbled.

"What if I tell you mine after, hmmm?"

Her eyes widened. "You fantasized about me?"

"Obsessively," I confessed dryly.

She smiled. "Okay, basically, I'm cleaning the cabin. It's a very hot summer day so I am wearing nothing but one of those French maid style, black and white, frilly aprons. Then you come in, you're shirtless, of course, and you take me from the back. Really hard … and … um … we don't use a condom."

I stared into her lovely eyes.

"I mean, I'm not saying I want to do that, or that I do that sort of thing. I'm super careful with my body. Funnily enough, it was my father who sat my sister and me down and taught us that when I was thirteen years old. Both of us were too stunned and weirded out to even be embarrassed. As a matter of fact, I haven't been in a lasting relationship since I was sixteen. Anyway, I couldn't even if I wanted to. I'm not on the pill. I know, I know, too much information. I always babble when I'm embarrassed."

God, she was such an innocent.

"Condoms have no place in fantasies," I murmur. "I wasn't wearing one either when I fucked you again and again in my head."

Her eyes widened with surprise. "You did."

I nodded slowly.

"How hot were you for me?"

"Like you wouldn't believe. I took you in every conceivable position. You don't even want to know some of them. They were that crude."

"But you were so cold and horrible to me."

"Put it down to pure frustration. I was fucking horny all the time, and I had to watch you bouncing around the place totally unaware of what you were doing to me."

She giggled. "Did you masturbate?"

"I might have. Did you?"

She blushed. "Yeah."

My eyebrows flew up in surprise. "What, down there while I was up here?"

"No, in the hot spring."

"While you were naked?"

"Of course."

"Go on, show me how you played with yourself."

"Later …" She raised her face to mine. Our lips connected and she slowly leaned back against the pillow pulling me with her, inviting me to explore her. God, she felt so damn good.

Her tongue dipped between my lips and I licked back, tasting her. She was soft and as delicious as warm peach. My hands slid down her silky skin. The need for her was screaming at me, but I didn't want to rush things. I wanted her, but I wanted her slow and easy.

She jerked her hips upwards and it sent an electric shock straight to the base of my spine. Damn. She was making this hard.

I buried my face in the valley between her breasts, but her scent brought me to the brink of coming. I couldn't resist licking her, tasting her. The sudden tremor through her body caused by just the simple touch from my tongue sent me crazy. Her head was pressed into the pillow, her throat exposed. It made me mindless with desire. Mindless with wanting to see her howl my name again erratically, while I pounded into her. I bit that soft space where her neck met her shoulder and she cried out. I snatched my pillow, and lifted her hips high enough for me to slip the pillow beneath her.

Then, I ate her pussy.

She pushed back at me as I licked and sucked and bit and worshiped at her altar of sweet sensuality. I pushed my tongue into her, as deep as I could get, licked the wet walls and she babbled like a mad woman and begged for satisfaction.

I moved lower and licked the tight ring of muscles. She jerked her hips uncontrollably. No one had done that to her before. She whimpered like an animal. I slipped a finger into her pussy, and inserted the slickened digit into her glistening entrance.

It entered easily. I added another finger and slid both in and out of her warmth. Her heat drove me crazy.

"Fuck me there," she said, as she lifted her hips and spread her legs even wider.

Oh Fuck. My dick jumped at the sight of her complete surrender. I pulled my fingers out, and positioned myself between her open legs. My dick jumped with impatience. God, she was hot.

The condom lay in its packet as I pushed my fingers into her pussy and used the slickness to coat my cock. I pressed the wet head of my erection at her tiny pink ring. Watching her face, I saw her slow down her breathing and relax her muscles. Her mouth parted in a gasp as the mushroom head went in, but then I was shocked by how smoothly her body welcomed me in. She sighed as I slid into her glorious heat.

I pulled out and pushed back in again and again, harder and deeper until I was balls deep. Only then I broke eye contact with her and looked down at our coupling. Her pussy was wide open and my cock was totally buried in her ass. The way her body was wrapped around me made me feel almost feverishly possessive of her. This woman was mine. This was my privilege and mine alone.

I dipped my fingers into her pussy and used my thumb to circle her clit.

Her eyes widened. "Oh, yes. Yes. Oh, yes."

I intensified my thrusts. Her passion matched mine and guided my movement, until I felt as if we were parts of a machine. Perfectly aligned and flawlessly in tandem. The heat and the tightness were indescribable.

Then she said the words that drove me over the edge. She begged me to own her. I fucked her like a crazed beast, until her head flung from side to side, her pussy gushed all over my fingers, and her mouth opened in a scream of bliss.

I clamped my hands on her hips and thrust even faster into her until I exploded. All that I was fused with all that she was.

Oh FUCK!

CADE

By the time we woke up again the sun was bright and fairly high in the sky. It looked like it was going to be a beautiful day. A day where it would be feasible to travel into town using these old mountain roads.

My normal routine of getting an ice bath in the creek, coffee and then tucking myself away in the workshop was out of the question. Today was the day I was supposed to take her into town to inquire about her car. Was this also the day I lost Katrina to the outside world?

A couple of days ago, that was what I thought I wanted. Now, even the thought of her leaving left me twitchy and restless. I wanted her to stay. At least for a little while longer, but what if she didn't want to stay? I knew nothing about her. She must have another life waiting for her outside this cabin. Like a proud fool I had rebuffed her efforts to tell me about herself or her life.

I needed time to think.

To make my plans.

I unthreaded my legs and arms from hers, gently smoothed her hair out of her face and pulled myself out of bed as quietly as possible. Just as I was descending the ladder, with our faces opposite each other she opened her eyes.

"Cade?"

All I wanted to do was get back into that bed, bury myself deep in her body, and tell her she was going nowhere without me. *Play it cool, man.*

"Hey. I'm putting some coffee on the stove. Want some?"

"Yeah. I never turn down coffee."

"Ok." I took another step down the ladder.

"Cade, wait …"

"What is it?"

"I just … want you to know that … I don't know what I'm trying to say here. Um, the weather is good enough for me to get into the town, isn't it?"

I kept my face expressionless. "Looks pretty good to me."

"I guess I should get out of your hair, huh?"

I went down the steps and started the fire in the wood stove for coffee. I think I was stunned. She didn't want to stay! It had to be karma. All my life women wanted to stay with me and I was the one kicking them out, pushing them away. And none too gently either. And now that I actually found one I wanted to stay with, she didn't want to. It would be funny if it wasn't so fucking painful.

"Hey!" Katrina stuck her head over the mezzanine. "Do they have any cute cafés in town?"

"I'm not sure about any cute cafés, but I sometimes get something to eat in Frank's diner. They've got Formica tables and paper napkin dispensers if that's what you mean by a cute café?"

"That'll do me. You want to grab some breakfast in town with me before we call about my car? I'm buying."

"Um, yeah. We can get some breakfast."

"I could kill for some hash browns right now. How long will it take to dig your truck out of the snow?"

"Not long. We need to boil the kettle to pour over the windshield. She likes to be warmed up like that before she starts."

She laughed. "Did you just refer to your truck as a female?"

"Yes."

"Does she have a ... name?"

"Yes, she does, but I will only tell you if you promise not to laugh at her. She's ... sensitive."

To her credit she kept a straight face. "Go on. I promise. No laughing. I'm dying to hear this!"

"It's Doris."

"Doris! Oh, my God. You are the most ridiculous mountain man I've ever heard of." Then she laughed that sexy, sexy laugh of hers and threw a pillow at my head. Of course, I got back up the ladder to my bed forgetting all about the coffee, or starting the fire under the stove.

CADE

Breakfast had moved into the realms of brunch by the time we were ready to leave. I dug snow out from around the truck tires while Katrina was still inside the cabin. She came out carrying some bags and stood next to the driver's side.

"Hey. I was just wondering, you know … er … well … what the *plan* is? Am I going to come back here with you later while someone fixes my car? I mean, should I bring my stuff, or come back for it?"

I stopped digging and looked at her, committing the moment to memory. She was beautiful beyond words. Everything about her was perfect. The woolen beanie she had jammed on top of her hair, the silky strands that had escaped and lay around her pink cheeks. The way she was licking her lips nervously.

She swallowed. "You know, is this it? Do we finish here, or do we buy more condoms at the village? I mean, I guess I'd just like to know where you're at with this, whatever this is between us. This is so embarrassing. I can't even speak."

"Do you want us to come back with more condoms?"

"Typical," she huffed, throwing her hands up in the air. "He's put it all on me! Surely, I haven't been too cagey about how I feel."

"Well, yes, actually you are being cagey. What are you saying?"

"I mean, didn't we have fun last night? And this morning?"

I smiled slowly. "Yeah, we did."

"Ugh. Men! Can't you just read between the lines of what I'm saying?"

"No."

"Do you want me to stay? Shall I just go now, or do you want me to stay with you out here for a while?"

"I want you to put your bags back inside the cabin and get more condoms in the town. Is that enough for right now?"

She beamed at me. "Yes."

"Alright."

"OK, fine."

There was an awkward silence. I think we both wanted to be excited about the step we'd just taken, but because we'd gotten tetchy about it with each other it was embarrassing to then bounce around in giddy celebration.

After a few minutes into the journey down the mountain Katrina started to giggle.

"What? What are you laughing at?"

"Us. We're so weird."

"What makes you say that?"

"We just are. This is the most random situation. I mean imagine anyone asking us how we met. 'Oh, you know I crashed my car and he rescued me from the freezing cold, and then we just … shacked up together. Like you do when you meet a hot mountain man. You're like a smoking hot, artsy kind of lumberjack. Every woman's dream!" she said throwing her head back and roaring with laughter.

She was right. We were totally weird.

"I've got to say, though," she added. "I've got plenty of girlfriends who will boil over with jealousy when they hear my 'love in a log cabin' story"

Love in a log cabin? It sounded so cheesy and yet so wonderful. "You're not really going to tell anyone, are you?"

She looked sideways at me. "Are you freaking embarrassed of me or something?"

"Ugh. No, would you please stop jumping to conclusions that are like three steps ahead of reason? Jeez, take it easy. I've been out here by myself for a long while now, you know. Suddenly, you're here, and don't get me wrong, I want you here. I like how it is with you around. Just … don't rush me. I don't want to think about shit like how we'll explain to people how we met. For one, I don't even like people."

She pouted prettily.

"I like you. Can we just keep it at that for now? Let me adjust slowly?"

"Fine, I won't tell anyone about us, okay. Sorry to hit a nerve."

"You didn't hit a nerve. I don't care who you tell."

We rode along in silence for a few moments until Katrina said, "You see, I told you we were weird."

I laughed. That was the thing about her that blew me away. Beyond how beautiful and sexy she was she was tough and kind, full of sweetness, and absolutely hilarious. She made me laugh just from being herself, and that was so fun to be around.

CADE

Frank's diner was more occupied than I'd have liked, but we found a booth towards the back. I sat facing the wall with Katrina facing out to the other patrons. Locals would assume she was just another skier tourist I had hooked up with. Very few people live here year round, so the inhabitants I see on my occasional trips to town have begun to recognize me and express casual pleasantries, much to my irritation.

"Hi folks, what can I get you?" Barbara, our waitress said. "Well, hi there, Cade. I didn't realize that was you!"

I took it as a bad sign that her usual polite smile had been replaced by a huge friendly grin, and grunted. As I feared she turned her attention on Katrina. "And who do we have here?"

I groaned inwardly. "Barbara, this is Katrina."

"It is sure nice to meet you, dear. I only ever see Cade by himself so you are a welcome sight for sure."

"Aw, it's nice to meet you too, Barbara."

Barbara turned back to me. "How did you fare through the avalanche? Everything ok up there at your place?"

"Yeah, fine. Didn't affect me too much."

Katrina looked from me to Barbara like she couldn't believe our conversation. "Um, apart from the fact that I crashed my car near his cabin and he had to take me in for several days? No, other than that it didn't affect him too much."

Barbara frowned. "Did you say you crashed your car?"

"Yes, ma'am. Up on Dogwood Pass right near Cade's place. My chains snapped and I went right over the edge. Cade heard it and came and rescued me. I was out cold. I would've frozen if he hadn't come for me."

"My goodness, honey. Well, you sure were lucky it was Cade that found you. About another mile up the highway and you would have crashed near old man Gafford's place and let me tell you right now, you do not want to set foot on that place."

"Why, what's the deal with old man Gafford?" Katrina said.

"Oh, he is just a misery guts. Hasn't got anything good to say to anybody. And anything that moves onto his property line, be it on four legs or two, he'll shoot at it. Just the most unfriendly man you're likely to ever meet."

"Well, I don't know. You could be describing Cade in another thirty years."

Barbara laughed and I cocked my chin to the side. I was not used to being addressed in such a familiar way, but I could see the funny side of it. Besides, her teasing was harmless and made me feel like she had accepted me as one of the locals.

"Is your car still up on the pass, honey?"

"Yeah, we're down here to get that taken care of today."

"Well, Cade, you know my husband, Barry, owns the garage, don't you? He'll get you fixed up if you go down there and see him."

"Thanks, Barbara. We'll do that."

As she walked away after taking our order, she looked back at me over her shoulder with a wink to say she approved of my being with Katrina. And the strangest thing happened. Instead of being irritated that she thought it was any of her business, I basked in the 'niceness' of her sentiment. And that was really strange for me. Even before I chose to live in the woods I had zero interest in being part of any community. People bored me. I found them nosy and presumptuous. Just because they knew who you were they behaved as if they had some investment in your life and had the right to comment about your choices.

Whenever I'd come into town since living out on the mountain, I avoided interaction like the plague, keeping my conversations to well-timed grunts and nods. Once you pass the stage of a grunt and a nod at someone, you've got to keep it up every time you encounter them. Much better when they assumed you're a cranky loner and kept their distance.

"This town is really cute," Katrina said. "It's got everything you need, but it's still cozy and friendly. I bet the people who live here are really happy."

"Don't tell me you'd like to live in a small town like this. I had you pegged as a city chick."

"No, no not at all. I mean, that's where I grew up, but that's not what I want for my life. I love these little pockets in the world where everyone knows your name and your troubles, you can always find someone to sit and have a coffee with if you come down to the town. There are families and old people, people who've lived here for generations and the tourists that breeze through dropping money and entertainment into daily life. I've always wanted to live in a community like this."

"Really?"

"Yeah, don't you like it? I mean, what brought you out here, anyway?"

There she goes again, digging up the back story. "If we launch into some big discussion now before I've eaten my steak we are both in for trouble. I'm an asshole when I'm hungry."

Katrina laughed at me. "Hey, I see that as progress. Good job, Cade, for letting me know that the jackass detector alarm bells are ringing. I will heed the warning."

CADE

The weather was nice so after we left the diner I went into the drugstore to get a jumbo pack of condoms and Katrina sat on a bench soaking in the winter sunshine. I stood at the doorway of the shop and watched her for a moment. It felt real, what we had. As she was already a part of my life. I couldn't really imagine life in these mountains without her any more. When she saw me she waved.

I walked up to her and she raised her face to mine and kissed me. Even though we were standing on the side of the street in a public place I wanted to lift her off her feet and take her right there.

She wanted to walk through town to Mitchell's garage. The sunshine felt good after a long winter. Symbolically it felt like it was thawing me out from the inside. Piles of snow shoveled off the sidewalks and roads were waist high and melting making puddles everywhere. It was a dirty mess, but Katrina laughed and called it charming. We passed the tiny, one room shop that the owner insisted on calling an art gallery, but was more like a tacky gift shop for the tourists and Katrina stopped in front of the window.

"I love this painting. It's so wild and colorful, but I actually recognize where this is. It's from around here isn't it? I could have sworn I passed it on my way here."

"Yes, I'm sure it is. They're all local artists' pieces in there."

"Really? Well, you should talk to them about your sculptures!"

I scowled. The last thing I wanted to do was sell my pieces. "Come on, let's get to the garage." I tugged at Katrina's elbow, but we only made it about five feet.

"Hey, Cade."

I turned around with a sigh. "Oh, hi, Paul."

"I'm glad I caught you. You haven't been in town in a while, have you? I got something to tell you. Come on in the shop, I want to show you something."

"Oh, we're in a bit of a hurry. I'll drop in the next time I'm in town."

"No, we aren't," Katrina said, and pulling out of my hand quickly followed Paul into his shop. Like she'd known him for years. I swear that woman did not meet a stranger. It was going to be very hard to live a hermit life with her around. Reluctantly I stepped through the doorway.

"Well, take a look around," Paul was saying to Katrina. "If you see anything you like I can give you a special price."

There were watercolor paintings of familiar local scenes, glossy black and white photographs of mountain wildflowers in the breeze, hand painted greeting cards with more mountains and flowers and the occasional totem animal. Nothing spectacular, and very far removed from anything I would ever have bought from a gallery.

"What's up, Paul?"

He walked to his desk, opened a drawer and took out a fat envelope. "Here you go."

I didn't take the envelope. "What's in it?"

"Your money. Eight hundred dollars. I sold your sculpture, Cade!"

I frowned. "What sculpture?"

He grinned triumphantly and strutted towards me. "The one Beau found outside your workroom. He told me you had trashed it. Said he didn't want any money for it, but thought it was too nice to be just thrown out. He was sure I could sell it and he was right. In fact, I was hoping you'd be in town after the storm cleared so I could ask you for some more pieces to sell."

At that moment, a phone rang from somewhere at the back of the shop and Paul pushed the envelope into my surprised hand, and disappeared through a low door, leaving Katrina and I alone.

"Wow! This is so great," she gushed. "I'm really happy for you. Don't you feel like celebrating?"

"Well, no, actually. It's really no big deal selling to the tourists. Everyone knows it's not actual art if you're selling from a one room shop in the middle of nowhere."

"Will you stop being such a damn snob? What the hell is the

matter with you? You could be doing a lot worse than selling your art to people who are trying to capture their vacation memories in an object. And having a nice man like Paul to deal your pieces for you. You need to pull yourself together, mountain man. There is no shame in you carving beautiful sculptures for a living. You think you can only be a true artist if you're having a show in some big city gallery. Be real, man. And stop being such a snob."

If Katrina had met me two years ago her accusation of snobbery would have been actually true. Eight hundred dollars would have paid for a bunch of exotic flowers ordered from a specialist flower boutique. She would not have recognized me in my handmade Italian shoes and my $75,000 bespoke Westmancott suits. I was a different person then. And if I was honest, one who would not have even noticed someone like her.

Paul came back out. "Sorry about that. Just the wife checking up on me." He rubbed his palms together. "Anyway, as I was saying, I get a steady stream of tourists in here, but the funny thing is I don't think I've ever had as many people show interest in one of my pieces as they did yours. People seem to love them." He made a face. "I kind of think I undersold it. I could have gotten a lot more. So if you have any other pieces that you would like to sell, just bring it in, or I could take a trip up to your place and have a look at what you have. I'll take everything you have. Big or small. Whatever you have." His eyes gleamed with the thought.

"Er ... no. I don't have any pieces for sale at the moment. If I do I'll bring them down." I grabbed Katrina's hand and started to pull her towards the door. I raised the envelope up. "Thanks for this."

He took a step towards us. "Are you sure I can't come up? There might be something that you don't think is good enough that might be salable."

"Nah. There's nothing. I'll see ya around.

"Paul, he'll bring them as soon as possible. I'll see to that!" Katrina said, as I dragged out of the door.

"What did you go and say that for?" I demanded.

"No reason," she said and began to walk off down the road. I shook my head. Beau, better have a good explanation for his behavior.

KATRINA

"**T**otaled? What do you mean?" I demanded with horror.

Mitchell, who owned the garage in town, had followed us up in his tow truck to where my car was wedged in the trees.

He shrugged. "I mean this car is not worth the money it will cost you to fix it. It's totaled."

My heart was beating really fast in my chest. I did not need this expense. It would throw all my plans in jeopardy. "Well, how much are we talking here?"

"It's difficult to say right now since I can't even get under the hood until it's out of the trees, but I'd venture a guess that since your front end is smashed to pieces it's going to cost more than the car's worth just to cover the body work. Not to mention whatever damage we find."

"Just throw out a ball park figure."

"It's over a thousand for sure."

"What? But I don't have a thousand dollars. Well, not right now anyway. I've got a few thousand coming to me soon. Can't you just fix it and then I'll pay you as soon as I can?"

"You're better off saving your money and buying another car when your money comes in," Mitchell said.

"Tow the car away, Mitchell. I'll sort some money out with you."

I was too distressed to answer. I just stood next to Cade as Mitchell sawed away the skinny pines that held my car wedged in. Then he hooked my car up to his tow truck. We watched as Mitchell drove away with my sad little car.

A long time ago I learned to see every situation in a positive light. If I applied that life lesson to this tragic scenario, I suppose the car could be a symbol of my life. Like he was pulling away all the old crap I'd been putting up with and clearing the way for something totally new in my life. I'd been focusing my mind on what I wanted, what I wanted around me, and this was all part of me starting over and having the life I always dreamt of.

"Come on, don't sweat it. You'll find something else to drive. I'll help you," Cade said.

"Yeah, I know. It's just a pain in the ass to have to deal with getting a new car. Ugh. Money problems make me so stressed."

"Oh really? Huh, money makes everyone on the planet stressed no matter how much or how little you have. Get over it because it's always going to be like that."

"Ha, says the man who comes from money."

His eyes narrowed, suddenly suspicious and dangerous. "How do you know I come from money?"

I stared at him in astonishment. With one sentence he had become a hostile stranger. It was almost as if I had never known him. I felt the color drain from my face even in the freezing cold. "I didn't. I was just guessing because you know, you're ... not really a mountain man. Your accent, your education. The way you throw your art away. When Paul gave you the envelope you didn't even open it. Actually, you looked like you didn't even want it."

Cade didn't respond. He went back to that veiled expression he had before I made him smile. Worry clutched my belly like an iron grip. Had I made a huge mistake by saying that? God, this man sends me to extreme highs and lows with ease.

"I'm sorry. I didn't mean anything by it. I'm just stressed about the money Having to shoulder this unexpected expenditure when everything is a financial mess for me right now."

He nodded. "Forget it. I'm sorry I attacked you. Let's just go back to the cabin."

The journey back to the cabin was mostly silent. I had no idea what he thought about, but I focused on how much money I would have to fork out to replace my car and how I would go about replacing it while I was up on the mountain.

When we got back in the cabin, Cade pulled me towards him. He put a finger under my chin. "Look, I have more money than I need. I'll buy you a car, all right. Obligation free. Call it a gift."

I couldn't speak. For some weird, totally crazy reason I wanted to burst into tears. I shook my head. I didn't know why I was refusing his money, but it just made me feel like such a piece of shit to accept.

"I don't need the money," he said softly.

I placed my fingers on his lips. If I could have spoken I would have told him then. Told him everything, but I couldn't speak and he scooped me into his arms and put me on the blankets in front of the stove where we'd made love before. Tears ran down my face. He looked surprised.

"Hey," he said. "It's not a big deal. I have no use for money here."

That just made me cry even harder. The iceman had a heart of gold. And I felt like a whore. He kissed my eyes gently and began to take my clothes off. He kissed every inch of my naked body until I was writhing like a snake with desire.

When he finally entered me, smooth and thick, I screamed his name, and raked my fingernails down his back.

Afterwards, I cooked two pieces of steak and tossed the salad I bought from town. After our meal, Cade built a fire and we toasted marshmallows. I think it was then, sitting huddled up next to Cade that I really began to understand the terrible, terrible mistake I had made.

KATRINA

https://www.youtube.com/watch?v=bnVUHWCynig

"How about a trip to the hot springs?" Cade said, when we woke up late the next morning.

I licked my lips. I couldn't put it off anymore. The issue weighed heavily on my mind, and all night long, I tossed and turned thinking about it. I had to be honest with him. No matter what the consequences. "But first, we should talk. I need to tell you something."

He sighed. "Can it wait until tonight? I've got stuff to tell you too."

My eyes widened. "You do?"

He nodded. "Yeah."

I smiled. "In that case, count me in."

"But there's something I've got to take care of first," he said, as he whipped the covers off me. I giggled as his rough beard settled between my thighs.

"Is your knee feeling up to a short hike? I can pull the truck up a little closer to the pools," he offered.

"That would be great, thanks."

There was a grin on his chiseled, bristly face and I wanted to devour and be devoured by him. He reached his hand across to my knee and pulled me down to his lap. Every little look and touch with him was fun and exciting. My heart started racing at the thought of being in the hot spring pools with Cade in the flesh.

"So, should we undress in the truck and make a run for it, or take our clothes off at the edge of the pool?" I asked with a cheeky grin.

Cade thought for a second.

"While the first idea has merit, I'd have to say that if you started taking off your clothes inside this cab I may not be able to contain myself and we may never get out of here. Probably best, if you really want that dip you should wait and take your clothes off at the bank."

I giggled. "Ok. Deal. We'll take our clothes off at the bank."

He parked the truck about fifty yards away from the pool and we sat in the cab soaking up the last of the warmth from the heater. "You go first."

Cade laughed, which I loved to hear. "No, we go together!" he said.

"Well, I think you are going to go first. Stand right over there and lay your clothes over that big rock next to it, and I'll sit here in the warm for another few minutes and admire the gorgeous view of mountains and pines and sun. I mean, this is a view you just have to soak up. The colors and the majesty! And man won't it look even better with you standing there buck naked in the middle of the vista."

"What? I'm not standing out there in the cold for you to ogle me!"

"Oh no? I've spent plenty of time being ogled by you, so go on now and get out there first. You'll get your reward of an eyeful in return. I just want mine first."

"Alright then. But you better not be too long." Cade opened the door and got out. Before he closed it, he leaned back in. "Don't dare fucking leave me out there long. I'm about to explode for you." He looked serious too. He really wanted me that much.

"I won't," I promised sweetly.

He took off his coat and hung it on the side view mirror. I watched him walk, that panther gait. So sure and confident. For an instant, I tried to imagine him away from these mountains. The life he must have lead before, but then he turned around and waved and the image was gone.

He pulled his sweater over his head, then unbuttoned his flannel shirt and laid them both over the rock I'd told him to. He turned to face me and let a smile light up his face. God, he was so beautiful, he made my chest constrict. He took off his shirt and brushed the skin on his chest and arms against the cold. Cade sat down on the rock and put his boots and socks in neat order next to his stack of shirts. He stood up again and unbuttoned his jeans.

I gripped onto the dashboard to steady myself.

He pulled his jeans off and stood there in his underwear. I guess he was hoping I would start getting out of the truck then, but I made him wait. I wanted to see everything.

Still in his underwear, he rubbed his hand over his erect penis. With his other hand he motioned for me to come on out. I shook my head. He dropped his underwear down to his ankles and I couldn't hold it any longer. I threw my coat off and started undressing in the truck as fast as I could. So that he would find the items later, I hung my bra over the rearview mirror and my panties over his gearstick. I didn't anticipate wearing any clothes for the short ride back to the cabin.

When I was completely undressed, I grabbed a condom from my bag. Cade had sank down out of view in the water. I forced myself to make him wait a moment longer. I was so ready to go for him.

I slowly opened the creaky door to the truck and lowered one bare foot down into the snow. Hell, it was so cold goose pimples scattered over my whole body, but my desire for Cade kept a warm glow in my belly. With more self-assured-ness, and more strength than I'd ever felt in my life I walked towards the rock pool.

Cade came up from underneath the water and watched me approach. At the edge I stopped to let the cold brush my skin a moment longer before I slipped into the warmth of the water. I reached up and untied my hair and let it fall around my shoulders.

Cade encircled my legs with his arms and pulled me into the water. I felt myself slide down Cade's body as we sunk slowly into the sensuous pleasure of the hot spring. He kissed me then, and I wished we could stay there in that magic moment forever.

CADE

"I'm starting to turn into a prune. Come on, let's get back to the cabin and sit by the fire now," Katrina said.

"OK, but I'm going to have to do some carving tonight. Since you arrived you've been nothing but a distraction to me."

"Are you complaining?" she gasped.

I hid a smile. "Ha!" I jumped out of the water and offered her my hand to help her out. Her body pressed against mine. She pouted.

"No, I'm not complaining," I said softly.

"Race ya," Katrina shouted as she slipped out of my grasp and took off stark naked. I watched her run towards the truck, completely ignoring her bruised knee. "Come on, just drive naked. It'll be fun. I've never driven in a car naked. Have you?" she shouted as she turned to look at me.

In the middle of winter? I shook my head. The girl was bonkers, but she made my heart smile. I picked my clothes off the rock. No, I don't think I'd ever driven a car naked, but why not?" It wasn't as if there was anyone around to see if I was stupid enough to sit buck naked behind the wheel in the middle of winter.

That would have been the case any other day of the year, except today.

When we pulled up there was a silver sports Mercedes parked in front of the cabin and my mother was leaning against the hood. She was dressed in a stunning, long cream mink coat, no doubt from her Russian furrier, and black boots.

"Fuck," I swore.

Katrina covered her breasts with her hands and squealed, "Who is that?"

"My mother," I muttered.

My mother turned then, and there was an incredulous expression on her face as she spotted us. Not surprising since we were both naked as the day we were born. I quickly got my clothes back on, but Katrina had thrown hers around haphazardly, so she was scrambling around searching for all the pieces with her ass up in the window. When she sat down to pull her leggings on my mother's stern, gravity-repellant face was staring at her through the passenger side window.

I buttoned my jeans and shrugging into my shirt got out of the truck. My mother was generally not good at smiling, but I was furious with her for deliberately staring at Katrina, instead of looking away like any other normal person would have.

"Come on, Mother. Let her get dressed in privacy," I said curtly as I neared her.

"Privacy?" she scoffed. "She should have thought about that before she took her clothes off out in the open."

I grabbed her by the elbow of her luxurious coat and guided her towards the cabin. She'd never been to my place before and looked around with undisguised horror.

"Oh, Cade. It makes me sick to think of you being out here alone all this time." She gathered up the hem of her coat so that it wouldn't come in contact with the dirt from my porch. When she passed through the threshold her long, thin hand covered her mouth in shock. "Oh, dear God." She looked at the rafters, the stove, and the clothesline across the room, the one and only bed on the mezzanine. She took it all in from the middle of the room then turned to me without saying a word.

"What are you doing here, Mother?" I asked.

Her lips thinned at my rudeness. I know she had driven a long way to get here, but her condescending attitude was pissing me off.

"I'm so sorry!" Katrina said, rushing in, out of breath and bumping into the doorframe as she pulled on her other boot. "So sorry about that! Hi, how do you do? I'm Katrina." She extended her hand to shake my mother's hand, but my mother filled her chest with air and gave Katrina an icy stare.

"Cade, this is not exactly how I expected to find you."

"Calm down, Mother. We're both adults."

"You said you needed space. You wanted to be alone to think about life. Instead you're playing naked games in the woods. Ugh, can she wait outside while we have this conversation?"

"Mother, this is Katrina. Katrina, Lynn. And no, she is not waiting outside in the cold."

"She didn't seem very cold a moment ago," my mother snapped sarcastically.

Katrina flushed bright red as she stood awkwardly by the door. There was an expression on her face I had never seen before. "It's not a problem. I can wait outside," she said, taking a step backwards.

"No, stay," I ordered firmly. "Anything my mother wants to say to me can be said in front of you."

"Cade, I want to speak to you in private. I don't even know this person."

"What do you need to speak to me about? Has something happened?"

"No, no it's nothing like that."

"Well, then what is it? What did you come all the way out here to tell me?"

"Cade, I'm shocked at your callousness. I'm your mother and I haven't seen you in two years. No calls or birthday cards! You didn't even come home for Christmas. We've had no communication whatsoever from you. And then to find you here living almost as a homeless person and driving around in the middle of winter without clothes, it's just unimaginable. Just look at that grown out beard. I've never seen you like this. Oh, I'm overcome! I feel dreadful right at this moment and I would think you would give some care to your mother. I haven't even been offered a seat! Do you even have one?"

Katrina pulled the stool out for her. "Here you go, Lynn," she said, but my mother looked at her with contempt as though Katrina was unfit to even address her by name.

"Is there somewhere else for you to go, young woman? I want to be with my son, not some—"

"Be nice, Mother," I interrupted, before the insulting name came out of her mouth. "Katrina lives here. You don't."

"Well, I've lived longer than you. I know her type."

"For God's sake, Mother. You didn't come half-way across the country to insult my girlfriend, did you? What do you want?"

"Your girlfriend?" My mother looked at me in shock. Like I had gone stark raving mad. Then she looked at Katrina, and back at me. Then she pressed her fingers to her temples and squeezed her eyes shut. "Oh, God," she muttered, her shoulders slumping.

My mother suffered from terrible migraines. She'd had them all her life. Ever since I was a boy I could remember her getting them and having to lie in a darkened room for hours, sometimes days. I moved quickly forward and guided her towards the stool. She sat down, her gorgeous mink trailing on the floor. I must admit until I saw that, a cynical part of me wondered whether she was being dramatic for effect.

"Have you got your medication?" I asked.

She shook her head. "But I have the prescription. Would you run into town and get it for me, Cade?" she whispered. "Otherwise, I won't be able to leave here before dark."

I frowned. "Are you sure you'll be all right, here? Do you want to come with me?"

"Oh, I couldn't face the winding road. I'll stay here with …"

"Katrina," I supplied.

"That's right, Katrina, and let me make it up to you and start off on the right foot with your new girlfriend."

"Are you sure about this?"

I couldn't believe my mother was being genuine, but then again she did move to New York when she was eighteen to tread the boards. She was a pretty good actress by all accounts until she married a rich, handsome, son of a property tycoon and found it much more enjoyable to live in luxury than to follow her dreams.

She patted my hand. "Yes, of course. It's my way of apologizing."

"Are *you* alright with this, Katrina?" I said.

She smiled weakly. "Oh, yeah. That's fine. Of course. Yeah, go and get your mother her medication. I'll keep her company."

"There that's settled then. Now, hurry back before it gets dark. It makes me nervous to think of you driving these terrible roads." She hands me her car keys. "The prescription is in the glovebox. You might as well take my car and leave that wreck of yours here."

My mother's sincerity was difficult for me to read and near impossible for anyone new to her acquaintance. She was not all bad though. Her good to bad ratio was just in constant fluctuation. And often when it looked like she was doing something out of meanness it turned out to be coming from a good place. Unfortunately, the opposite was also true. In that moment all I could do was cross my fingers and hope she was not up to something bad.

I prepared to leave and Katrina caught my arm. She looked deep into my eyes and said, "Please hurry." Under her breath, she said, "I had a great time with you today. The best."

I frowned. "I'll be back in less than two hours."

She looked like she was blinking back tears.

"Do you want to come with me?" I asked.

She turned to look at my mother then back to me. "She doesn't like me," she whispered.

I turned to my mother. "Maybe I should take Katrina with me."

"You will absolutely not leave me out here by myself. Katrina and I will stay. Go on now, Cade, it's not like I'm going to carve her up into little bits and pieces! We girls will be fine, now go on!"

Katrina smiled. "Of course, she's right. I'll be fine."

"She's a bit of a dragon, but she won't harm you." I kissed Katrina's cheek and whispered to her, "I'll be back as soon as possible."

"I'll miss you," she said. It didn't seem like a joke. I think she really meant that she'd miss me while I was gone. It was the craziest thing, but hell, I would miss her too.

KATRINA

HTTPS://WWW.YOUTUBE.COM/WATCH? V=XVVAYD3X5KA

A s soon as the door closed on Cade, Lynn stopped holding her temples and craned her neck to look out of the window. She waited until she saw Cade get into her car and drive away before she spoke. I guess she didn't want to chance him coming back in and overhearing our chat.

"Why are you here?" I asked. "I thought I was supposed to let you know when the job was finished."

She stood and examined the ends of her luxurious coat. "Isn't the job done?"

I bit my lip. "Not really."

She looked up, a mocking smile on her face. "That's not what I heard. I heard my son was kissing you on the street yesterday. And if your little naked drive in the mountains is anything to go by, I think your job is done. In fact, you might have even gone too far. You'll miss him? That's laying it on a little thick. No wonder my son thinks you're his girlfriend!"

"Well, I am his girlfriend. It's not an act!"

Her eyes glittered. "That is not the deal we had, young lady. I hired you to bring him back to us. Would you like to look over your contract again to refresh your memory? I just happen to have a copy right here," she said, pulling an envelope from inside her voluminous coat that looked very familiar, but I felt as if it was signed in another lifetime.

"God, no! I don't need to look at it again. I remember what it says."

"Oh really? Then why are you talking about being his girlfriend. I cannot believe how royally you've messed up. I told you to bring him back. You've done the opposite and tried to move into this shack with him. And you've got his mind turned around and warped out of all recognition. You have totally screwed this up."

"I'm really sorry. I don't know how this happened. When I agreed to do this, it was just … different to how I imagined it would be. I mean, it was a job, I definitely didn't expect to fall for him, but I have."

Her eyes narrowed and for an instant it reminded me of Cade. "Is it more money you're looking for?"

"No, absolutely not," I cried.

"Because it sounds very much as if you're fishing for more." Her voice was cold.

"No, Lynn, listen to me. Keep your money for all I care. I only did it to help my sister anyway."

"Oh, spare me the sob story. This is an absolute disgrace, but I'm going to pay you in full because I always keep my end of the bargain and I expect you to do the same."

"Listen, I just want out of this now. Forget the money. I don't want Cade to ever know that I agreed to do this!"

"Well, I'm afraid it's not that simple."

Lynn went back to look out the window. She held our contract and thumbed through it. I felt disgusted at myself to think of what I had signed up to do.

The 'job', if one can even call it that now was enough money to pay for my sister's surgery and care. I've been working two jobs, teaching and dancing in the club for two years now just to keep my sister in the facility she's in. They take care of her, but she needs the surgeries to remove the lesions on her spine, and secondary surgeries to address the muscle injuries caused by her paraplegia. I would have done anything to give her that.

So, when Lynn's agent presented me with the proposal to help get her son back among the civilized in exchange for enough money for me to help my sister and give up lap dancing, I couldn't believe my luck, let alone pass the opportunity up. It seemed perfect at the time. I wouldn't be harming anyone. In fact, I'd be helping a man who was lost to his family and the world.

"We don't have much time. My driver is on the way," Lynn said.

"What?"

"I need you to go back to where you came from. Next week the sum we agreed will be transferred into your account."

"I can't just go like that. What about Cade?"

"Cade is no longer your business. You have completely

ruined everything and gotten him even further entrenched in this nonsensical idea of living in the mountains. When he comes I'll tell him that you just couldn't take another minute in this awful place with no Internet connection to post your little pouty pictures, or selfies, whatever you call them on social media. If you agree to go now, even with your colossal screw up of our contractual agreement, your payment will still stand."

"Lynn, I don't think you understand what I've been saying to you." I crossed the room to face her by the window. For once, I felt confident in myself. My feelings for Cade overrode the feeling of intimidation I felt from women I perceived to be my betters. Like the mountain lion did to me, I looked right into her eyes so she could see my power. "Whether you like it or not I *am* Cade's girlfriend. We've fallen for each other. Cade wants to be with me and I want to be with him."

KATRINA

https://www.youtube.com/watch?v=2FkdleIkFyo

"You might be able to trick my son, but not me. I saw you coming a mile off. You're just after the money. Do you think I did not have you fully investigated? I looked into your family. You don't have anything. Or anybody! You're nothing."

"Tricking him? It's you who is tricking him. Using me to bait him out of the mountains. Did you ever take a moment to think of what he wanted? How can you do that to your own son?"

Her chin rose haughtily. "I did it because I love my son. Is this a life for a man of his talent, capability, and wealth? He is rotting away here. He has a family who loves him, beautiful homes, great wealth, important work, friends who care for him. His whole life was put on hold after the accident. It's time he came back to where he belongs."

I looked at her speechlessly, at how sure she was that she was making the right decision for her son.

"Have you even thought about what you're doing? Were you planning to live out here with Cade, all alone in this tiny cabin, no jobs, no friends, not ever seeing your poor, sick sister?"

I hadn't thought about how long we would be here. It did worry me to be so far away from my sister. Up here, we were too far away to make regular visits. I lifted my chin defiantly. "Cade and I haven't exactly figured all the details out yet. We're just at the beginning of our relationship."

"Or is your plan, which is much more likely, to milk as much money out of this entanglement with my son as you can? Waving your tits and ass around for money just like you did with all these other men?" From that coat of dead animals Lynn brought out a stack of photos. She didn't give them to me. Deliberately, she threw them all over the floor.

Pictures of me dancing in the club with folded up dollars tucked around my thong and stockings were everywhere on the floor of the cabin. Taken in secret, the pictures were dark and dingy, but unmistakably me. There were pictures of me giving lap dances, and the worst were the ones where the men who paid extra so that I would touch them. She even had pictures of me working with another girl at the club. We were in the middle of a special room in the back, up on a platform with several men in chairs around us. A bachelor party. We do a lot of those.

My friend, who I worked with on these gigs, and I split the money, and it was enough to pay rent for the month in just a half-hour. We kiss and pretend to writhe around together on the spinning platform so the guys get a good view of everything.

They just want to see us feel each other and get off on it. It's all a show. We were performing an act, and just thinking of the money. Whenever I had to do those gigs I went into my own world in my mind and kind of even forgot the guys were there.

Except now, I was looking at these pictures and I could see the faces of the men watching. There were so many faces in those pictures. All watching me writhe for them.

All with the same look in their eyes. I was only there to satiate a need in them. I had no other use to them. I had no life outside their hard on. I was there for no other purpose than for them to cum over.

Suddenly, I was on my knees trying to pick up these degrading, disgusting pictures that were scattered across the backdrop of where my love for Cade began. I felt like dirt. Tears started to roll down my cheeks as I scrambled around picking the horrible photos up.

"There now, don't cry. Come on, let's get you out of here before Cade comes back and sees you like this."

"But, I love him."

Lynn laughed. "Hush now, darling. That's the most ridiculous thing I've ever heard."

"But it's true. I really love him," I insisted.

"Look at this picture." Lynn crouched down by me and held a picture up in front of my face. It was of me giving a lap dance to an enormous man in every sense of the word. He was over a foot taller than me, and a big eater. He wore gold rings on almost every finger and a fedora hat over his bald head. He was secretly wanking himself behind me. "Does this look like a picture Cade would like to see? If I show this to him, do you think you'll still be his girlfriend?"

Hot tears ran down my cheeks onto the photographs. Shame rose up in my belly. Every cell in my body cringed. What have I done to myself? I could never bear to let Cade see me like that. I couldn't see the light die from his eyes.

"My son needed time and space. He's had that. It's time for him to come home now. And, my dear, even if you follow him back to his life, you just won't fit into the world we live in. Everyone in our circle is educated, wealthy, and exhibit more than class than you appear to have. All Cade's friends belong to our set. You'll know you're different. They'll know you're different. You'll feel that the others in Cade's circle don't like you. They'll always whisper about you. You'll feel embarrassed, which is understandable, but then Cade will start to feel ashamed of you, and that's what will hurt you the worst."

"But what if we stay out here in Colorado?" I said through a wash of tears.

"No, this is not his life. He has a life. A business. He just fell apart and needed to be alone for a while. That is over now, partly thanks to you."

"I love him."

She blinked. I could see she was losing patience with me. "Cade has responsibilities in New York. He's coming back with me, and if you try to stand in his way then ..." She rifled through some of the photographs still on the floor until she found the one she was looking for. "Ah, this is one of my favorites." She held it up and talked about it like it was a picture she was really proud of. "Cade will be shown this photo and all the rest of them."

I refused to look at the photograph. "And what will he think of his own mother when you reveal all? Maybe I should just stay right here until Cade comes back and we'll see how he reacts to what we've both done."

She stepped closer, amusement glittered in her eyes. "You imagine he would choose you over me? A whore who opened her legs for money."

"Can't you understand that I love him?"

I saw it in her eyes. How she changed tack. "Honey, you're young and beautiful. You have your whole life ahead of you. Take this money, which is probably more than you've ever seen at one time in your life, and likely never will again. Help your sister. That's very noble of you and then start over. Just start over. Go wherever you want, and do whatever you want. There's more to life than you've known so far, which is why you've fallen for Cade. You've never known someone with decency and class before so even a sullen hermit living alone in the wilderness is like a chink of light coming through to illuminate how terrible your existence has been up until now. I promise you, you'll thank me one day." Lynn patted me on the back like we'd just played a game of tennis together, "There's a lot of other fish in the sea. Cade's just a little bit out of your reach right now."

I was heartbroken to hear what she said. Somewhere after I crashed my car I totally lost sight of what I was supposed to be doing, lost sight of my place in the world, and romance clouded my mind. I felt like such a fool.

"Come on." Lynn helped me to stand up, picked up my tacky bag and held it out in front of her like she was afraid of what germs might be on it. As if by divine knowing a car drove up at that moment. "There, your ride is here now." She guided me towards the car.

As we passed the fire pit outside, I stopped. There was a little tiny piece of carving lying near the pit that Cade had been messing around with the other night. I wasn't paying much attention at the time. I picked it up and ran my finger over it. It was the mountain lion. He'd carved the majestic face of the lion we'd encountered on the mountain together.

"Tell him I'm going to write him a letter and explain everything. Will you please tell him that?"

"Katrina, darling, you're embarrassing yourself now. You signed an NDA. You cannot tell anyone anything or you'll end up behind bars. Now, be a good girl and get in the car."

"You won't show him the pictures, will you? Please?"

She shook her head. "As long as you keep to your side of the bargain. I won't."

"I'll keep to my side of the bargain."

"Then he will never see them." She smiled at me then. A polite, cold smile. "Goodbye, Katrina."

CADE

I drove the Mercedes fast on the winding road. It would be dark in a couple of hours and I didn't even want to think of my mother on these dangerous roads once it got dark, but I was desperate to get back for another reason too.

Something felt wrong. I felt it in my gut. Something about Katrina felt off. Ever since my mother arrived I felt the change. Almost as if she had become suddenly opaque to me. Maybe I was overthinking and she was just embarrassed to be caught naked by my mother, but I really wished my mother had never turned up.

Why she came now after two years was a mystery.

I switched off the engine and headlights, grabbed her medication from the passenger seat, and jumped out of the car. Quickly, I strode over the snow towards the cabin.

Even then I knew.

I knew before I opened the door that Katrina was not in the cabin. I don't know how I knew, I just did. The place was already empty of her warm, beautiful presence. I pushed the door and my mother was sitting on the stool waiting for me.

"Hello, darling," she said softly.

"Where is Katrina?" I demanded from the doorway.

She shrugged. "She had to leave."

"She had to leave?" I repeated incredulously. "On foot?"

My mother laughed, but it was a forced, artificial sound. "Don't be silly. Of course not. Robert came and picked her up."

I scowled at her, my mind running in circles. "Robert, your driver?"

"Yes."

My face turned to stone and for a second neither of us spoke. We stared at each other. Then she spoke.

"I'm your mother. I miss you terribly, Cade darling. Is that so bad? Does that make me a monster? Of course, it doesn't."

She was not suffering from migraine. I had been sent on a wild goose chase. I closed the door and stepped into the room. "Mother, you better tell me everything. Start at the beginning and don't miss a single detail."

My voice was so cold, I saw her shiver.

LYNN

I looked at my son. This was the child I carried in my own body. My boy. My favorite child. All my life I'd subtly manipulated my whole family, made them do the things I wanted. I had my migraines, I had my tears, I had my position as the real power behind the throne.

But now something had changed.

He had changed.

I had miscalculated.

She had made him change. Impossible to imagine, but he had fallen for that two-bit stripper. But the feeling was new and the ropes she had tied around his heart were still green and tender. I could damage them. I could rip them off. I just had to play my cards right. I just needed to move cautiously.

I wrung my hands together. There was no expression on his face and his eyes were hostile. Never had I seen them icy like that.

"You'd been away for two years, Cade. Two years. What was I

supposed to do? Let you waste the rest of your life here on this mountain? Take a good look around you, Cade. Is this any way to live? What is the point of living like this? All your money rotting in banks. I'm your mother. Ask anything of me, but don't ask me to let you live here in this horrible cabin."

"What did you do, Mother?"

"I hired her."

His eyes narrowed. "As what?"

"I hired her to come here and show you that there is more to life than being a hermit."

"She crashed her car."

"I didn't ask her to do that. All she was supposed to do was get here before the storm so you would be forced to let her stay for a few days."

"And then what?" His voice was so quiet I had to strain to hear.

"I told her to use whatever means at her disposal to bring you back to civilization."

"You thought having sex with a woman would do that?"

I could feel the heat rise up my throat. "Well, you used to like it."

"So why did you come here, if she was supposed to be doing the job?"

"I found out something about her."

"What?"

"These." I held the photographs out to him. Right at the top of the pile was the one with the guy masturbating while she did her lap dance.

He took it from my hand and looked at the first one. I saw him flinch in shock. When he looked up, his eyes were bleak. "How did you come by these?"

"After I hired her, I became suspicious of her intentions. So I hired a private investigator, who dug up these photos. Most of them are open source."

The photographs were crushed in his fist. He was breathing fast. "So you came running up the mountain to scare her away."

"I was thinking of you."

"Bullshit, Mother. Bullshit."

"You can believe me or not, but I love you. Nobody will ever love you as much as I do."

He appeared to be controlling himself, as he turned away from me and looked out of the window. "You better go back down the mountain before it gets dark, Mother."

I realized that he was furious with me. Even when he was just a child, he got very quiet when he got really angry. My other son and daughter would shout and scream, not Cade. His fury was disturbing because it was so controlled. I could feel now his anger was barely leashed. It radiated out of him in waves and yet, to a complete stranger he would seem to be just polite and courteous.

"I'll go, but promise me you won't be mad at me. I was just trying to help. Maybe I was wrong to interfere in your life, but I had to do something. I was desperate. You are my son. I would do anything for you."

"I'm not angry with you, Mother. I feel sorry for you. You will never understand. Now, please go. The roads get dangerous as dark falls." He walked to the door, opened it, and walked out. I stood for a moment in the middle of the cabin. He would come around. He always did. He was my son.

Then I followed him outside. He was checking my tires to make sure the chains were still on and safe. My son loved me. One day he will forgive me.

She was not right for him. I knew that from the moment I met her. I knew I was playing a dangerous game and I was right. She was bad news. But I got rid of her. I stood at the driver's side door.

"I'm sorry, Cade. I'm sorry it didn't work out. She looked like such a nice girl. How could I have known?"

"Drive safely, Mother."

I got into the car and he stood and watched me drive away. I watched him in the rearview mirror. He just stood all alone staring at the car as it disappeared from view. I must have driven for at least five hundred yards when I heard that terrible, terrible roar. It bounced off the mountains and echoed all around me.

I slammed my foot on the brake and listened, but there were no more sounds after that. A sob was torn from my throat. Dear God. What have I done?

That was my beloved son calling for his mate.

KATRINA

I didn't pay much attention to my ride back. I sat very still in the back of the car and gazed unseeingly out of the window. I kept imagining what Lynn would tell Cade. In my heart, I knew she was going to show him the pictures. How else would she stop him from coming to me? I tried not to imagine his face when she showed them to him, but I kept on seeing it. How disappointed he was. He had come to trust me and I betrayed him. He would think I slept with him because of the job.

If Lynn had not come I would have confessed to him.

In fact, I was ready to tell him in the morning, but he said to wait until later because he had something to tell me too. How I wished I had not agreed to wait. I should have insisted that we just get it over with.

Maybe he would have been angry but he would have forgiven me. He would have looked into my eyes and my heart and known I never meant him harm. It was not such a bad thing, what I did. I did it for my sister. I never meant to hurt him, but now that Lynn was in charge of framing the story, I would have no chance.

By now she would have painted me as some cheap whore.

Oh, those pictures.

I buried my face in my hands. If only I had told him this morning. I would have told him that I never meant to sleep with him. The agreement I had with his mother was simple. All I was supposed to do was attract him. Make him feel he was missing something by being on the mountain. Make him want to re-start his life in the city.

Never was sex part of the equation, but I couldn't help myself.

I was so insanely attracted to him. He was so different from the cold, sophisticated, beautifully dressed, perfectly coiffured man in the photograph that Lynn showed me. In that photo, I saw an extremely handsome man, someone so completely out of my league that I even said to Lynn when I met her at that hotel that I didn't think I could bring someone like him back from the edge of a self-imposed solitude, but she assured me that I had all the qualities that he admired most in a woman.

She told me she chose me from hundreds of photographs. At that time, I saw a totally different side to her. She seemed warm and friendly and helpful. I told her what the money was for, and she asked about my sister and showed what I thought was genuine concern. I even went as far as to think I was helping her. I wanted to do my best for her, but all that time she just thought of me as an expendable tool. Some throwaway dreg of society.

W hen we arrived at my apartment, Susie, my roommate was in. She was making one of her famous ham, cheese and French mustard sandwiches.

"My God, what happened to you?" she asked, as I came through the door.

I wanted to be strong, but the look on her face made me burst into tears. She left her sandwich and came up to me and hugged me. "Hey, hey, whatever it is, it is not as bad as you think, remember?"

I'd heard that line so many times, more than I care to. Every time something bad happened to us we told each other that, and it always made me feel better, but not this time. This time I'd really fucked up.

"I fell in love with him, Susie."

"Oh shit."

She went to the fridge, poured me a big shot of Vodka, and topped it with orange juice. "Here, get this in you."

I took a sip, but it didn't even taste the same. It felt cold and tasteless in my mouth.

"Want to tell me what happened?" she asked, plopping next to me on the sofa.

I nodded and poured my heart out to her.

"What a fucking bitch," she said bitterly when I finished.

"I think you should leave it alone for about a month, and

then you should make contact with Cade," she said. "I don't think those photos are as disgusting as you think they are."

I shook my head. "You should have seen them, Susie. They were horrible. Truly horrible. When I'm at the club, it feels normal, just another job, all of us are in the same boat, but those photos. They were the pits."

"You know, people like that bitch, really make me angry. She thinks she's better than you because you're a lap dancer, but guess what, she needed you to get to her son. You were good enough for her then, weren't you?"

"I feel so ashamed," I whispered.

"Don't you dare let her make you feel ashamed of what you did. Are you telling me you won't do that all over again for your sister?"

I blinked at Susie.

"Well, are you so ashamed now of dancing that you won't do it all over again for Anna?"

I shook my head.

"Exactly. You didn't do anything wrong. You didn't cheat anybody, you didn't harm anybody. You just used your God given body to dance and give pleasure to some lonely men in order to help your sister. Hell, I admire you."

"I cheated Cade."

"No, you didn't. It was a job, Katrina. What do you think spies do every day? It's their job. Besides, as soon as you had feelings for him, you were going to tell him, weren't you? If she had not turned up today, you would have told him, wouldn't you? Because ... you are honest like that. Unlike her. Who has probably lied to Cade again."

Tears filled my eyes and ran down my face. "I love him, Susie. I've never felt like that about anyone before. Ever. I love him so much it hurts. It actually hurts," I sobbed.

"Oh, sweetie. I'm so sorry. You don't deserve this."

I blew my nose. "I don't know what I was thinking. Of course, I couldn't have him. He's a billionaire and I'm just a lap dancer."

"Stop it. Stop that. You're a good person and he's not like his mother. He gave up all his wealth and went to live in a cabin by himself. He wasn't looking for a socialite. He knew you had no money. He saw what kind of junk heap of a car you had and yet he wanted you."

"He was so nice he said he would buy me a car," I wailed.

"See. He cares about you too."

"Do you think so?" I just wanted to hear her say it even if it wasn't true.

"You're beautiful, Katrina. Inside and out. Don't forget that. Lynn can pretend now that you are some cheap whore, but she chose you out of hundreds of women because she knew what you had. And there's something else that you need to remember too. I believe she's afraid of you. She was afraid that her son would fall for you and that's why she came running to the mountain the moment she got wind that her son was seen kissing you."

My hands were clenched so tight, the knuckles showed white. "Do you think he could have fallen for me?"

"Absolutely, and she knew that too. That's why she had to get rid of you as soon as she could. Even before you had done the job of bringing him back to civilization."

"What shall I do now?"

"Look. Don't do anything just yet. Everything is a mess right now. Let the dust settle. You're supposed to get the money next week, right?"

I nodded.

"I don't think she will dare cheat you. So go to work as normal and wait for the money to hit your account first. We'll sort Anna out and then we'll see what we can do about this situation, okay?"

My heart felt so heavy, but I nodded my agreement. Maybe I couldn't have Cade, maybe that would just remain a dream, but for now I had the money for my sister and that was what I should focus on.

CADE

HTTPS://WWW.YOUTUBE.COM/WATCH? V=NCBAST507WA

I sat in my black Lamborghini in the parking lot of the club where Katrina worked for an hour running over my decision. A minute for every picture my mother gave me of Katrina. I saw red when she first put those pictures in my hand. I wanted to physically lash out and hurt her when I saw the first one, but I didn't. I clenched my teeth so hard my jaw ached.

My mother began to cry.

Maybe they were crocodile tears, but I'd learned my lesson. Even the worst psychopath had their own breaking point. I was responsible for Christine's breaking point, I didn't want to be responsible for my mother's. My mother had a long journey ahead of her. I didn't want it to be on my head that she didn't arrive home safely.

After she left, I didn't look at the photos.

I burned them in the stove. All of them.

They made the place stink so much of ink and chemicals I

had to open all the windows and doors. It had started snowing again, but all the magic was gone. It was no longer a refuge. I looked around and saw it through my mother's eyes. The cabin looked small and joyless.

I picked up my tools, went to my workshop and got to work with a mad man's intensity. For two days and nights I carved, only stopping to eat and snatch a couple of hours of sleep.

I thought a lot during all those hours alone about what I wanted out of life, what mattered to me and what didn't. As much as I wanted to push Katrina out of my head, I just couldn't do it.

She was always on my mind.

I thought of the movie Manhattan, when the character played by Woody Allen was lying on his couch and talking into his tape recorder. He led himself to the question of why life was worth living. For him it was, Groucho Marx, Willie Mays, the second movement of the Jupiter Symphony, Louis Armstrong's Potato Head Blues, Swedish movies, Flaubert's Sentimental Education, Marlon Brando, Frank Sinatra, the incredible Apples and Pears by Cezanne, the Crabs at Sam Wo's and finally ... the face of his love, Tracy's face.

Each of us had our precious things.

The things that made us care. The things that made us human. For me, the list was even more sparse than Woody Allen's. Before Katrina came my life was empty and mean-ingless. I spent weeks sculpting something only to destroy it.

To me: Katrina's face was everything. She made me a human being again. So what if my mother had paid her. I know we had something. Something more than money. Something rare and precious. I didn't care if she danced for a living in the past. I cared only about the woman I knew.

When the carving was finished, I loaded it onto the back of the truck and stood looking at my cabin. Truly I had loved it. It had saved my life when my life seemed worthless and death was preferable. But that time was over.

I said goodbye to the mountain and left.

I went to see my mother and got the address of the club where Katrina worked. As I was leaving she ran out of the house and held me tight. "Please don't think badly of me, darling. I did it all for you. Because I love you," she said. I knew then, she hadn't been honest about everything. Whatever it was I would find out when I found Katrina.

So, now here I was: Parked in my car outside the club where Katrina danced. Katrina was in there for sure. I knew because I called ahead. I was not storming in there to find she was not even on shift. It was not a very mountain man thing to do to check ahead, but Katrina was right, I was a total poser of a mountain man.

A leopard didn't change its spots.

I was a billionaire.

I never took chances.

I always went for the sure thing.

I had planned to go in, sit on the periphery not to attract too much attention and just drink a beer, check out the scene. I'd planned to take it easy and slow, hang out for a while, and let her see that I was there. Once she'd spotted me across the room, I figured she'd come over, throw her arms around me and kiss me.

Her boss would get mad and fire her in front of everybody to which she would respond by flipping him the bird and rolling out her wonderful laugh with an arm slung around me, as we headed to the door. That was how I imagined it would go, that we'd take our time with it.

The reality of the situation played out very different.

I walked up to the doormen and they parted like the red sea to make way for me. They were all smiles. I didn't even have to pay at reception. The benefits of arriving in a luxury sports car. I was whisked into an enclosure marked VIP. This was before I'd uttered a word. It was dark and cool with a loud stag party in progress. Already a plan was forming in my head.

A waitress in a long black dress with a long slit up one thigh arrived. I ordered champagne. The best the establishment had. I asked if Katrina was working.

She smiled. "As a matter of fact, yes. I think her slot comes up soon."

"I'd like to have a private dance with her."

Her smile lost some of its glitz. "Well, I believe Katrina is no longer doing private dances, but I'm sure any of the other girls will be glad to oblige."

"But I only want a private dance with Katrina," I said.

She cleared her throat. "If you'd like to wait I'll get the manager for you and you can discuss it with him."

A man in a black cut suit came hurrying towards me. He had

sad eyes and a long pale face. He beamed at me effusively and repeated what the waitress had already told me. I took my JP Morgan Palladium Visa card out of my wallet, put it on the table, and pushed it towards him. It was made of actual palladium and gold and had no spending limit. His eyes widened the way a fisherman who suddenly found a prizewinning catch at the end of his line would.

"I'm prepared to spend an insane amount of money in this establishment for the privilege of one private dance with Katrina. Shall we start with a bottle of champagne for every dancer in this place ..."

He gulped, his Adam's apple bobbing. "Of course. I'll ... I'll arrange something for you, Sir."

KATRINA

https://www.youtube.com/watch?v=DfIcZtjAch8

I traced my finger along the edge of the dressing room as I waited for my turn to come on. I had one stage performance left tonight. Two more days and I'd have Cade's mother's money. Then I was finished with this job.

The door opened and the manager slipped through.

"Hey, Arnie," I greeted his reflection in the mirror.

He smiled broadly, which was surprising, because Arnie was one of those gloomy people. The glass was never half full, it was always half empty in his world. He was a wet blanket, but I liked him. He stood by me a lot in the past. Whenever I couldn't make it, when I needed some extra funds, he was always there for me.

He scratched his left hand nervously and I turned around on my stool to face him. "What's up, Arnie?"

He cleared his throat. "Instead of the stage show can you do a private dance?"

I frowned. "No, I told you I don't want to do those anymore, Arnie. Get someone else."

"Listen, the man asked for you."

I froze. "He asked for me?"

He nodded enthusiastically. "Yes."

"Does he have a beard?"

"No. Clean shaven. He's a smooth operator. Arrived in a Lambo."

He could have shaved. "What's his name?" I asked eagerly.

"His credit card was engraved with Mortenson."

My heart sank. It wasn't him. "Please will you do it. As a favor to me."

I shook my head. I was so disappointed I could cry. "Please, Arnie. Get someone else. I wouldn't be able to dance. I'm just not feeling it anymore. He'd be wasting his money."

He took a step forward. "Please, Katrina. If you do this you won't even have to come in for the next two days and I'll let you keep the whole price of the dance. In fact, you don't even have to pay the house fees today."

I stared at him in surprise. "What?"

"Look. Just do this dance. I'll sit in the surveillance room myself and if he even lays a finger on you, I'll have him thrown out. Just do this for me. As a favor."

I stared up at him. Wow, Arnie must really rate this guy. He's almost begging me to do this.

"Please, for all the times I've helped you out," he cajoled.

I sighed. "All right. But I'm warning you now, if that guy tries anything, I'm breaking his fingers."

He grinned. "Don't worry. I'll have the bouncers outside. One wrong move and ..."

"Fine."

"I'll show him to B5 now then?"

"Okay. I'll go there in a couple of minutes."

"Thanks, Katrina."

"It's okay. You've helped me a lot and this is nothing, I guess."

We smiled at each other. In a funny way, I will miss him. He's a good guy at heart. I turned around and looked at the mirror. I wasn't sleeping very well and there were dark circles under my eyes that even make-up couldn't hide properly. I slicked on a layer of gloss and stood. I was wearing a long shimmery green dress and I smoothed it down my body. I turned around and gave myself a last look before I walked out of the dressing room.

I stood in front of the door to B5 and took a deep breath. Instead of being reluctant, I should be happy. This was my last performance. After this I knew I would never again dance for money. I grasped the handle and opened the door.

My eyes met Mr. Mortenson's and all the air rushed out of my lungs. He was leaning back, relaxed, his knees far apart.

There was a bottle of champagne in an ice bucket and two glasses on the small table at the side of him.

My heart was beating so fast. Without his beard he looked unknowable, unreachable, and yet an unbelievably beautiful stranger. He was what Arnie had said. A smooth operator in a suit that cost more than what I could make in a year.

Then the music came on. *You walked into the party like you were ...*

For a second I did nothing. Then I closed the door and did what I have never in my life done. I pressed the button that stopped the surveillance camera. It was what the other girls did when they wanted to earn a few extra bucks. I didn't want to earn extra, I just wanted some privacy. I saw his eyes flick to the button and I could see he understood what I had done.

I opened my mouth to explain everything, and Cade shook his head. "Dance for me, Katrina."

So I did. I danced in a way I had never danced. With my heart on my sleeve. I shimmied out of my dress. When I let the bikini bra pop open I leaned close to his face. As I had known he would, he captured a nipple in his mouth and sucked.

"Cade," I moaned. I really wanted to give up then and just let him take me, but I didn't. Instead, I turned around and with my hips only inches from his face, I bent from the hips, and dragged my little black thong down my legs.

I sighed when I felt those big, callused hands grab my hips and I felt his tongue swipe all the way up my slit.

"You're so wet."

I couldn't say a word. All I could do was focus on the way his tongue felt as it slipped into my pussy. I ground my pussy against his mouth, trying to find relief, but he had other plans. He moved his mouth and kissed the inside of my thigh and slowly licked the skin. I had no choice but to stand like that, ass in the air, while he hungrily sucked and licked, and finally, when I thought I would melt into a pool of quivering flesh, he made me climax.

Then he turned me around. I watched as he unzipped his trousers. He didn't have to ask. I spread my legs wide, and willingly sank down on his bare cock. I had missed this. Oh, God, how I had missed having him inside me.

"Hell," he growled, when I was so completely impaled on him that it felt as if he was in my belly.

He looked into my eyes. "Fuck, Katrina. You look fantastic. Bounce on my cock, baby."

I held on to his shoulders and slowly rose up. The cream from my pussy made his cock glisten. It was so sexy. At first I made short, shallow plunges then, my slam down began more and more violent, until I was going all the way down. Until I was burying his cock inside my body.

It felt so damn good to be filled and stretched by him. Then he grabbed both my breasts in his hands and squeezing them tightly, he sucked both my nipples at the same time. Now that my nipples were both securely in his warm mouth, he moved his hands away. Then his fingers began to play with my clit. I nearly screamed with the pleasure overload. My breaths were coming hard and fast. I knew I was almost there again.

"Let yourself go, Katrina," he groaned.

With a moan I went over, my pussy milking his cock as he began to spurt into me. I rested my forehead against his chest as I waited for my breathing to come back to normal. I could hear his heartbeat. Fast and hard. I could have stayed like that forever. With his thick cock inside me, knowing it would be hard again soon, and he could ravage me again, but I knew we had to clean up and get back to reality. We needed to talk. Slowly, I slid upwards, his cum leaking out of me. I wanted to stand, but he kept me in his lap and slowly inserted two fingers into me. All the way in. He watched his fingers go in and out of my body. Then he brought those fingers coated in both our juices to my lips. Looking into his eyes I captured them and sucked them into my mouth.

He pulled his fingers out of my mouth and inserted them back into my pussy, then he brought them to his lips and sucked them the way I had. He closed his eyes with the taste.

He caught my hand and put it on his cock and I could see that he was hard again. "Go get your coat and meet me at reception. We're leaving," he said.

I stood up then, dressed quickly, and opened the door. Instead of walking through the club I decided to take the steps up the stage and then out through the back. It was the fastest, shortest way out.

CADE

After she walked out of the door I cleaned up quickly and stood. If I didn't know it before I knew it now. Katrina was mine. She was not working in this joint for another second. I opened the door and I saw Katrina on the edge of the stage. It was clear she was trying to get to the stage door.

But as she was nearly there, a man who had been sitting on his own said something to her. I couldn't hear what he said because I was too far away, but I saw her face react to whatever he said and I felt fury slam into my gut. It must have been something sick, dirty to make her that upset. She said something back to him, again inaudible to me and he stood up angrily. And by the way he stumbled slightly, I could see that he was more than a little drunk.

I began moving towards her.

She never saw me.

The man pointed at her. "Come back here, you little bitch!" he shouted at her.

By then I was running towards them. He lunged at Katrina and caught her by the ankle. She got one good crack in with a punch to the side of his head, but he was so drunk she could have hit him with a two by four plank and he would have still been standing.

He pulled at her from the stage. I wanted to kill the asshole.

She screamed and everything seemed to kick into slow motion. I felt her scream echoing around me as she toppled and fell backwards. Lunging forward, I caught her fall. And then, there she was, right into my arms, again. She looked up at me, but in the confusion and shock didn't instantly register how I got there. "I got you, babe," I whispered in her ear. By then, the bouncers reached the situation and tackled the idiot. Even so, I was tempted to kick him in the guts. I had to tell myself, I got what I came here for, to stop myself.

With Katrina in my arms, I marched out of the club with as much conviction in my decision as when I took her from her car and carried her to my cabin. There was chaos going on all around us, but I was completely calm.

Outside, in the cold air I set Katrina down and, taking off my jacket draped it around her shoulders. She put her hand on my face. "I miss your beard." She sounded shy, unlike how we were with each other.

"It's easy enough to grow back."

"No, I think I like you like this too."

I chuckled, and suddenly she hugged me, wrapped herself in my arms and started crying.

"I'm so sorry, Cade. Everything just got so screwed up. None of it was supposed to turn out like that, I promise you. I'm so sorry."

"It's alright. I'm here now."

"I thought I'd never see you again," she sobbed into my chest.

"I'm sorry it's taken me so long. I needed to get my head together."

"I'm not a whore. I was never meant to sleep with you. I just couldn't resist you." She pulled away and looked deep into my eyes. "You need to know that I did it for my sister. That's why I do these jobs. She needs constant care, and I won't see her go without."

"It's ok. It doesn't matter. Nothing matters."

We held each other outside in the cool night air for a long time. It felt so good to hold her close to me. It wasn't the most romantic spot to reunite with drunk men wandering past every now and again, but it was perfect.

"Can you come with me to my hotel room?"

"Now?"

"Yeah, we need to have a talk."

"OK, I'll come with you."

CADE

When we arrived at the grand hotel I had booked into she looked up at me, a strange expression in her eyes. "Is this the real you, Cade?"

"This is me, but that man you shared the cabin with is me too. You think you can cope?"

She bit her lip and smiled. "Yeah, I can cope with anything as long as you're there with me."

The concierge held open the door and we walked through. "Good evening, Mr. Mortenson," the bellboy greeted.

"You don't have the same name as your mother?" she asked.

"I do, but I imagine she gave a false one."

She nodded. "I guess she showed you the pictures."

"Yes."

The lift doors swished open and we stepped in. I kept my hand on the small of her back. I wanted to slip it lower, but I knew where that would lead. We had to talk first. I needed to get to the bottom of this mess. I had things to confess too. Things I had never told anyone.

We reached our floor and the doors opened. We walked down to my suite and put my card key into the slot. As soon as we entered the room, Katrina turned to look at me, her eyes moving worriedly over my face.

"Cade, are you alright?"

How did I start talking about the things I needed to tell her? I felt there was a huge knot of rope in my stomach, which I didn't know how to unravel. "Yeah, I'm fine."

"It's just that you look like ... I don't know."

"No, I'm alright. I just have to tell you something terrible. I know the words I'm going to say ... even for them to pass my lips ... will make me sick. But you have to know about it, and once you do then we can talk about 'us'. I mean, if that's what you want. You may not want anything to do with me once you've heard my story." I took a deep breath. "I know how I feel about you. I haven't been able to get you out of my mind since you left. I'm hoping you feel the same way, but—"

"I haven't been able to stop thinking about you either. I've missed you like crazy. The truth is I've been brokenhearted without you, Cade. Besides, I've been worried sick about what you would think of me after seeing those pictures. So whatever it is you have to tell me, it's okay with me—"

"Please, stop. You just have to hear this other part first before you tell me anything like that." A wave of emotions crashed over me and I had to sit down with my face in my hands. My eyes were burning and my voice shook. The old, buried emotions were stirring around in me like some kind of internal tornado. It was terrible and scary and more powerful than me.

"I'm here and I'm listening. Take your time." Katrina knelt down beside me and rubbed her hand over my back.

"The short version of the story is that I am a horrible monster of a man. What I've done is …"

"Cade, stop it. Whatever you've done it's going to be ok. I mean, look at me dancing for those disgusting men. I'm sure whatever it is that you want to tell me; it's just as bad as my past. Listen, our pasts will cancel each other out." She put her arms around me to comfort me, which actually made me hurt worse. I pulled her arms back so I could look in her eyes.

"Did you ever wonder what brought me out to that mountain? To that cabin all alone?"

She smiled. "I thought maybe you were trying to get away from your mother? Is that not it?"

Katrina brought a smile out of me. "I wish it was that simple."

She scowled and looked at me anxiously. "Are you in some kind of trouble with the law?"

"No." I took a deep breath and began at the beginning. "I don't know what you know about me, but I worked in the financial sector. I built nothing, I created nothing. All I did was buy and sell other people's companies. In a fraction of a second I and my super computers could make millions of dollars. I was a vampire. Sucking the blood, sweat, and tears of ordinary people. But I didn't see that. Not at all. And neither did the people around me. Like me they thought I was a big deal. I was invited to the best parties and feted at all kinds of industry events."

I paused and stared at the carpet, the little star pattern on it.

"I absolutely loved the high of a big kill, and I was good at it. Very good at it. I can safely say that my life was my work. I was a workaholic. I worked all hours of the week and most of the weekends too. Even after I got married."

"Oh God." Katrina sat herself down on one of the new chairs. "You're married?"

"No, I'm not married. Not anymore. Just listen, please."

The color had drained from Katrina's face. "I'm sorry. Go on."

"Christine and I were from the same background. We dated and when she became pregnant we got married. Stupid decision. Looking back, we never should have gotten married. It definitely wasn't a match made in heaven and I don't think I ever even loved her. I guess I allowed myself to be influenced by my mother on that one. Anyway, without love the marriage floundered very quickly. It was mostly my fault. I was always absent. No one could have had a relationship with me. Almost as soon as the twins were born we became strangers, but I didn't leave her. I didn't want her, but I didn't want any other women either so for a few years we carried on. I left her to get on with it and concentrated on my business. I was earning so much money and had become so influential I was invited to attend the Bilderberger meeting. The children were growing and happy. Oh, God, I can't talk about this!"

I got up and kicked the leg of the armchair with frustration.

The shame and anger I felt towards myself swelled up all over again. I was back in that time. I hated the words I was going to have to say. I took a few deep breaths and turned to Katrina again.

"Go on, Cade. Say it. You're scaring me."

"I'm sorry. Don't be scared. I've just never told anyone this before, and I hate this part of me."

She stood up and touched my hand. "You saw those photos of me. I hate that part of me."

I sat down on the sofa next to her, but I couldn't speak. She thought the photos of her dancing for men was bad. She had no idea. I buried my head in my hands.

"Oh, Cade," she whispered.

"My children," I said, and my voice broke.

"The twins," she prompted.

I nodded. "A boy and a girl."

"Are they with their mother? You don't see them?" Katrina asked.

I shook my head. 'No.'

"Why?" she asked, and there was a new dread in her voice.

"Because ... because ... one night ... I came home from work really late." I stood up and walked away from Katrina. I went to stand at the window. I looked into the dark sky and I let myself remember that night.

CADE

Two years previously.
https://www.youtube.com/watch?v=2shR99NnwCA

I came home as usual and walked through the door, and there was an odd smell in the house. The smell of something that had been burnt. I walked through the empty house and I could see that Christine had set the table with candles as I passed the dining room.

Ah, it was dinner that had been burnt.

I frowned. I knew I hadn't missed a dinner date.

I went upstairs taking the stairs two at a time. I went straight to the children's room. They were both asleep. I kissed their soft faces. I knew I was missing out on too much. I could see just by how much space they were taking up in their little beds that they were growing fast. I loosened my tie and decided then that it was time to make some changes to my life. I didn't want to completely miss out on their childhood. I went to our bedroom and Christine was sitting by the fireplace. She'd been drinking, her eyes were glazed.

"Well, well," she slurred. "Look what the cat dragged in."

"I'll sleep in the guest bedroom," I said, turning away.

"That's right, run away. Little coward," she taunted.

I whirled around. "Why do you drink if you can't handle it?"

"Why do you drink if you can't handle it?" she mimicked. "I drink because I'm *unhappy,* Cade. Because I'm so damn unhappy."

I felt nothing. "Do you want a divorce?"

"Divorce," she shrieked. "That's your fucking answer to everything, isn't it?"

"Well, if you're so unhappy with me and this arrangement doesn't suit you, I would have thought the best solution would be to get divorced. I'm not exactly jumping for joy at our situation," I said reasonably.

She flew out of her chair. "You're not jumping for joy. Could have fooled me. I was under the impression that things were exactly how you wanted them, you godless, heartless man. You've got your position, your work, your money, a wife who is begging for a little love from you, two beautiful children. What more could you ask for?"

I shrugged. "Peace of mind when I get back from work?"

It was as if I had detonated her nuclear button. She went insane. She ran at me screeching like a witch, her face contorted, her fingers extended and ready to rake her nails down my face. I caught her and held her easily. "Calm down, Christine. Calm the fuck down."

As soon as she stopped kicking and screaming and became still, I let go of her. She stepped back and looked into my eyes. Hers were filled with hatred.

"I'll ask Stephen to start to draw up the divorce papers tomorrow."

"It's so easy for you, isn't it?"

"I don't understand you. You hate me. You're unhappy and yet you don't seem to want a way out. What do you want?"

"I want you to love me," she cried.

I looked at her in astonishment. Did she not know? You can't make yourself love someone. You either feel it or you don't, and I don't. I never have. "I'm sorry, but I don't love you, Christine."

She shook her head. "What a fool I've been. Throwing my love at you. Well, enough is enough. Go on. Go and sleep in the guest bedroom. Have a good sleep."

I stood there for another moment and then I turned around and walked towards the guest bedroom. Really, I slept so much there most of my clothes were there anyway. It was nearly one in the morning, but I still had some work I needed to finish so I lay on the bed, propped up on pillows and fired up my laptop. In no time I was so completely engrossed with the figures on my screen I almost didn't hear the engine of a car start up. But in the silence of the night, it jarred on the edges of my consciousness. I left my laptop on the bed and went to the window. I was just in time to see my wife driving away.

Instantly I knew what she had done. I ran to my children's bedroom.

She had taken both of them.

I phoned her.

When she picked up the call she was crying so hard she was sobbing.

"Christine, come back. Let's talk about this," I said as calmly as I could, even though my heart was pounding with fear. In the background I could hear my son start crying.

"Shut up," she screamed at him.

"Christine. Look, just come back. You've been drinking. You shouldn't be driving."

"Come back for what?"

"Just come back. I'll change. I'll be different."

"You're a liar, Cade Mortenson. A big, fat, liar."

"Please—"

The rest of her words were cut off by a blood-curdling scream and the sound of a crash. For a few seconds I couldn't even move. I couldn't believe it. The phone never cut off. I heard the whole thing. I couldn't let go of the phone even though the sounds I heard were horrific. They will never ever leave me. I can't ever get those sounds out of my head. I screamed her name and I heard a raspy breath. Then she said. "I hope you're happy now."

Adrenaline pumping through my veins, I called the police while I ran down the stairs. I jumped into my car and sped down the road. I didn't get too far. I slammed on the brakes and every nerve in my body felt like it was on fire.

Her car had collided with a ten-ton truck. It was so crushed it was unrecognizable. I didn't run. I walked towards the smoking wreck in a daze. I already knew no one could have survived it.

What I saw I would never forget for as long as I lived.

KATRINA

He cleared his throat and tried to get hold of himself while I tried to keep my face from showing my horror. I don't think I was successful. I couldn't even begin to imagine what he had gone through must have been like. I would rather dance for a million men than go through that.

"I was careless," he whispered. "She was right. I was a heart-less monster. I cared only for myself. I should have seen that she was at breaking point. I never should have let her go. If only I had cared enough in that one moment everything would be different right now. My girl could sleep through anything, but I could hear my boy crying in the background. I blame myself for their passing. It is my responsibility to own and rightly so."

"No, it's not your fault," I cried passionately. "You were not the one who got into a car while you were drunk. You didn't crash it."

He turned to look at me with tortured eyes. "Yes, it is my fault. She was going to her mother's. Another three miles and she would have made it. If only I hadn't called her she may have made it."

"We'll never know, but I know this much. Terrible, terrible accidents happen every day. Things that crush our souls, things that we have no control over. This is just one of those things."

He ran his hands through his hair distractedly. "Talking about it has brought it all back, Katrina. I don't think a day will come when I will be able to feel less guilty. I don't know if I can live here with people. It was better when I was up on the mountain."

"Why did you come down from the mountain then?"

"Because I had to find you. Without you the mountain was impossible."

I smiled. "Then I will come up to the mountain and be with you. How about we live on the mountain and attempt to negotiate society bit by bit, huh?"

He nodded. That blanket of sadness around him would not shift. Maybe it would never shift, but I knew I could bring him happiness. One day we would have kids of our own. One day, I would bring him back to civilization.

One day, I would make it all right again.

I walked up to him and lay my cheek against his chest. "I don't know much about you, and I hardly know your history, but I know I love you, Cade," I whispered. "You are not someone I met a few days ago. You are my soulmate. I've always known you."

He circled me with his arms. "I don't know if what I feel is love, my heart has been frozen for so long, but this thing is so strong, I'm willing to climb mountains, cross seas, and die for it."

I looked up at him with tears in my eyes. "If that is not love, I don't know what is."

"In that case, I love you, Katrina." He stopped and scratched his chin. "Shit, I don't even know your last name."

I grinned. "It's Katrina Black."

He smiled softly. "It doesn't matter I guess. It won't be Katrina Black for much longer."

My heart felt as if it wanted to burst out of my chest. "We'll take it step by step, okay. One day at a time. We have all the time in the world."

He touched my lower lip. "You know, sometimes I thought of you as an angel. The way you appeared out of nowhere and brought such joy and light into my world."

"Actually, my stage name is Angel. I come out in a little white costume complete with wings."

He smiled. "Suits you. Sometimes looking down at you sleeping below I felt like Silas Marner looking at the golden hair of the child he found and thinking he had found his lost gold coins again. You are my lost gold. It's your challenge if you choose to accept it."

"What's that?" I asked curiously.

"The challenge to keep me from turning into old man Gafford. If you stay with me, I'll be less likely to turn into a miserable old mountain hermit. Are you up for it?"

I smiled. "Oh, it's not going to be that hard to cheer you up. I've already figured out how to do that and I've only been with you for a few days.

He looked deep into my eyes. "Yes, that you have done."

"Before we do anything else, I want to tell you about what happened with your mother first, and then I want to tell you about my sister."

We talked for hours, and hours, and hours that night, and the next night, and the next night …

EPILOGUE

KATRINA

One Year Later

"It all looks so beautiful," I breathed, looking around me in wonder. My sister had made the most beautiful arbor for us to stand under for our marriage. Then she found some guys to place it near the creek and tied fresh wild flowers from the mountain around it. Tea light votive candles hung from the top of the arbor. It was rustic and simple and beautiful.

"You're not just saying that? I mean, you could have had the grandest society wedding America has seen in forever. Better than Kim Kardashian's wedding."

"Which one?"

"OK, OK," she said with a laugh.

I looked into my sister's eyes. They were sparkling with health and I had to swallow hard to stop myself from crying.

After her first operation, she opened her eyes and thanked me. She told me I was not her sister, but an angel sent by God. I shook my head and told her she was the angel sent by God. If she had not been sick I would not have taken Lynn's job. I never would have met Cade. And my life would have been that boring humdrum existence.

"Yes, I promise you this is exactly what I wanted," I said, leaning forward to kiss her cheek. "As long as you are here to see this then I don't need anyone else but Cade to be here."

She laughed. "Fine with me. If you're happy, then I'm happy."

"I am happy. Wildly, unreasonably, incredibly happy."

She grinned. "Ok."

"Come on then, I need to get into my dress."

We waved at Big Bill and left him waiting outside the cabin. Big Bill was the only guy in town ordained to perform marriages. I think he went to some kind of spiritualist group to be given the right, but whatever. He was a really nice guy, and was endearingly happy to come out and perform the ceremony for us in exchange for a few freshly caught trout from the creek and a bottle of homemade gin.

Yup, I made the gin. I found out I have a special talent for making moonshine.

We went into the cabin. Did I mention that the cabin looks completely different now? Cade increased it to double its original footprint. I insisted on one thing though, that we keep the sleeping arrangements above, exactly as it was when I first arrived. For some strange reason, climbing into bed with Cade at night always gives me a flutter in my stomach.

Sometimes it makes me a bit sad that we no longer live here full time.

Cade announced one summer morning that he was done hiding on the mountain. He wanted to start a brand-new life and he was going to move the sculpture of me that he made when we first met from the cabin back to our home in the city. It was the first piece he had not thrown away or destroyed. He told me he planned to, but when he lifted his axe he simply couldn't do it. Something in him had changed forever.

So Cade and I started to spend more and more time in the outside world. Only retreating here when we wanted to be with only each other.

Then one day, while we were out fishing, he got on his knees and proposed. Saying yes was the easiest decision I ever made. Actually, it wasn't even a decision. I always knew he was my fate. From the moment I opened my eyes and saw that bear of a man my heart always knew I'd bitten off more than I could chew.

And it was right. There was no chewing this one.

This one swallowed me whole.

Without Cade knowing, I had a wedding dress made for me by a little old lady in town. A gorgeous, simple white dress with a sweetheart neckline and scoop back. It was perfect. Simple and beautiful just like everything else around me, and what existed between Cade and I. Anna helped me into it, then she pinned flowers in my hair.

"Oh, my God, Katrina. You're so beautiful."

"If only Mom and Dad could see us now."

"They're looking down on us, Katrina. They're looking down on us," she said softly.

Tears filled my eyes then. "I love you, Anna."

"And I love you more."

When I walked out of the cabin and down the path to the arbor by the creek, Cade turned to look at me. The expression on his face when he saw me in my white dress will be engraved in my memory forever. I saw him blink back tears and then, of course, I started crying, like a damn waterfall. Thank God for waterproof mascara.

He put his thumb under my chin. "You're my life."

I knew then that we may not always have happy moments in our life together, but these good ones are so good they could outweigh any bad life could throw at us.

Later tonight, I will tell him about the child growing in my belly.

EPILOGUE II

LYNN

"I don't know why you are moping around. You should be dancing with joy. You got Cade off the mountain, which is what you wanted, isn't it?" Mason, my youngest son said heartlessly.

"He's marrying a stripper," I snapped.

He laughed. Unlike Cade who always cared whether he made me happy or not, Mason didn't give a damn.

"What's so funny? You're not embarrassed to have a stripper for a sister-in-law? All our friends must be laughing at us."

He shrugged. "I can see why he likes her."

"Don't be disgusting."

Mason laughed again. "Don't bust a gut, Mother. He's happy. Plus, he's forgiven you for what you did, which I think is very big of him. I don't think I would have."

I ignored the jibe. "If he's so happy, why have I not been invited to that, that pagan ceremony she calls a wedding."

"Probably because of what you just called it."

"What would you call it? Up there in the wilderness, with no family around. The man who is officiating is not even a preacher. I can't believe my oldest son is doing this to me."

"He's not doing anything to you. He's just living his life. Don't you think he deserves some happiness after what happened to him?"

"Yes, yes, of course, but does it have to be with her?"

He sighed. "You're going to have to make peace with her soon. I have a feeling we're going to be hearing the pitter patter of little feet soon enough."

I slumped into my chair. "Maybe they'll break up."

"Don't count on it. Last time I had dinner with them, Cade was well and truly gone and so was she."

My spine straightened. "When was that?"

"A month ago."

I looked at him reproachfully. "And you never thought to invite me?"

Mason smiled. "And ruin a perfectly good dinner. No."

I scowled. "I don't know what I did to deserve sons like you and your brother."

Mason stood. "Right. I've got to go."

"Where are you going?"

"I have a very interesting date to attend."

I felt a bit sour. One son had deserted me and the other was going on an interesting date. "Who is it?"

"Well, it's a sassy woman who is looking for a fake fiancé to take her to her ex's wedding. I had nothing better to do so I volunteered."

I closed my eyes. I could feel a headache coming on.

The End
Mason's story. Coming soon.

NANNY & THE BEAST

CHAPTER 1

A pril

The address was only a short walk from the Knightsbridge tube station. The sun was shining as I took the little path that led to the private square called Little Sion. In no time I was standing in front of a large set of wrought iron electric gates adorned on either side by stone lions. Before I could press the intercom button, a voice with a foreign accent brusquely instructed me to go through the small side gate.

Okay.

As I got to the gate it clicked open. I pushed it, and walked through. Standing on the asphalt driveway for a second, I looked up at the mansion. Wow! Painted brilliant white, it practically glinted in the sun. As if it was some ice palace from a fairy tale. Who'd have thought such a massive palace existed right in the heart of Knightsbridge.

A huge bald man wearing an earpiece and a black suit that was a size too small for him was making his way towards me. The guy was so big the top of my head came up to his tree-trunk biceps. Of course, as basic human interaction demanded, I smiled politely at him. He did not smile back as he let his eyes dart over me suspiciously.

Okay. Be like that then.

"I've come about the job. I have an appointment with Mr. Volkov," I said.

He grunted. "I know. Come with me."

He turned on his heel and I fell into step beside him. Actually, it was more like a jog, or to be even more accurate, a fast-paced sprint. Damn him.

"My name is April Winters, what's yours?" I gasped, in an effort to be civil and pretend the speed we were travelling at was my normal pace.

He grunted again, before his eyes slid down to me. The expression on his face did not change. "Brain," he said.

I mean, I could have said, 'what', or laughed outright, or if I wanted to carry on being polite and civil, 'pardon me', but I kinda knew I'd heard right. Somehow the name suited him to a T. Of course, he would be called Brain.

I gave up any pretense civility at that point, and silently followed him up to the house.

Two more 'brains' in black suits watched us from the entrance of the house. They wore the same expressions of extreme distrust. For the first time, I wondered what the hell I had got myself into.

Who was my employer?

Obviously, the first thing I did when I was told I had been selected to apply for this job was Google Yuri Volkov. All I found were images of an extraordinarily handsome businessman escorting beautiful women to high society parties. No mention of a palace in Knightsbridge, or goons that behaved as if they belonged in a bad Mafia movie.

Come to think of it now, in every photo I found he was unsmiling, giving me the impression of a cold, aloof man. Not that that bothered me any.

I would be in charge of his niece and report her progress to him. And that was all I would be doing. Since I was extremely good at my job, I didn't foresee needing to take shit from Mr. Volkov.

There was one picture of him though, playing polo in Windsor, which caught my attention. Something about the expression in his eyes as he leaned down to swing his mallet. Here was a man who got what he wanted. An implacable man. A man you did not antagonize.

A man you allowed into your body.

Did I just go there?

I crushed the thought.

I was a professional, and I had no intention of ever being anything else. Under no circumstances was I exchanging my good reputation for any man. No matter how hot he was. Besides, as if a man like that was going to give a woman like me even a second look. All those beautiful women swarming around him like flies to shit. Not a chance.

Which obviously was a good thing.

The last thing I needed was temptation.

Not that I was saying I was tempted.

The man opened the grand doors and my jaw dropped. Jesus! Mr. Volkov must be a very, very, very, very successful businessman. The interior of his abode made me feel like I had just stepped into an episode of The Secret Lives of Billionaires. It had one of those foyers with a spiral staircase. From the glass ceiling four floors up, hung the biggest chandelier I had ever seen in my life. It seemed to have millions of crystal pieces that caught the sunlight streaming in from the top and practically blazed like it was on fire.

Our shoes rang on the marble floors. Some poor minion had polished them so hard I was afraid Brain would be able to see up my skirt. Fortunately, he kept his eyes ahead. We turned into a room, which I suppose could be called a music room, since there was a gleaming grand piano in it.

"Wait here until you are called," Brain said.

There were two women sitting on the fine chairs in the room. I recognized one of them. Mary Sedgewick from Caring Nannies. She was generally accepted as their best asset. She looked at me with a smug expression. The other woman, I didn't know, but I guessed she must be from Sarah Bright's agency, because she was holding a file with their logo on it. She nodded at me formally.

I smiled at them both and took a seat on one of the armchairs. It was upholstered in sunshine yellow and was incredibly comfortable. Funny thing. I was suddenly nervous. I took a mint out of my handbag and popped it into my mouth.

A middle-aged woman in a severe navy-blue suit came into the room. "Ms. Sedgewick, please come with me."

Mary stood and with a confident smile walked up to her. The door closed behind them, and I turned my attention to the French windows. Outside stone steps led to a formal garden that seemed to stretch endlessly. There was a fountain. I stared at it blankly. Ten minutes later the woman in the navy-blue suit was back, which surprised me. Maybe Mary didn't get the job, after all.

"Miss Winters," she said with a smile.

I smiled back, stood up, smoothed my skirt over my thighs, and walked towards her. She introduced herself as, Mrs. Misha Gorev. She was Mr. Volkov's personal assistant.

If this job was not Mary's, I felt confident it was mine.

I was good at my job. They called me the child whisperer back at the agency. I had tamed spoilt, rich kids; brats with behavioral problems; sick kids. So far, no kid had defeated me. I straightened my back as Mrs. Gorev's hand closed over the intricately carved, gold door handle. The door opened and the wind left my lungs.

Good Lord! It must be the devil himself sitting behind the desk, because only the devil could be that darkly handsome.

CHAPTER 2

Y^{uri}

As the door opened, I looked up from the file in front of me. Beyond Misha was the next candidate. My eyes found hers and for a second my brain stopped working. Two things:

First: she looked *nothing* like her photograph.

Second: lust. Pure, unadulterated lust flowed like fire in my veins.

God, I wanted that broad!

She smiled and it was the sexiest thing a woman had ever done with her lips. Actually, she looked like she belonged in a Raphael painting. Huge green eyes, flaming red hair, and skin like thick cream. My gaze ran down her body. Even in the cheap shirt buttoned up to her neck and loose gray skirt she was sexy as fuck.

I leaned back in my chair making it tip back. "Come in and take a seat, Miss Winters."

She walked, a sure feline glide, towards one of the two chairs in front of my desk and sank into it. "Thank you."

Her voice was soft and mysterious.

"So, tell me about yourself?" I invited, trying to keep my eyes from wandering.

"Well, there's not that much to tell. I am a teacher by profession, but I decided that I preferred working with small children, so I became a nanny."

"Why?"

"What do you mean?"

"Why do you prefer working with small children?"

She shrugs. "I don't know. Nobody has really asked me that. I think it's because I love their innocence. I find them honest and easy to deal with."

"You don't like dealing with adults?"

She shifted in her chair. "Not so much."

"Why not?"

"Like I said. I find people often have hidden motives, and they are not very honest most of the time."

"So you like honesty."

She looked at me directly. "Always."

"That will be all, Miss Winters." I stood. "Thank you for your time."

She did not stand. "That's it?"

"Yes, Misha will contact you on Monday and let you know the outcome of the interview."

Her eyes widened. God, they were fucking beautiful. I felt my cock twitch and come alive. Definitely: I made the right decision. She is far too distracting to be working in this house. I do not need that kind of temptation.

She stood suddenly, her eyes flashing. "Why do I need to wait for Mrs. Gorev to let me know? Be honest. Just tell me I haven't got the job. That way I won't have to stress about it over the weekend."

I nod. "Very well. You didn't get the job."

"Why?" she demanded.

I smiled. I couldn't remember the last time anybody questioned me this aggressively. I was not sure how I felt about it, it niggled at my sense of absolute authority and control, but I was intrigued. Very intrigued. "Do you want me to be honest, Miss Winters?"

"Naturally."

I walked around the desk, and she took a step back. The move was instinctive and told me clearly, the lust I felt was not one-sided. She wanted me too. We faced each other, and I felt it instantly. We were natural born adversaries. We'd fight like cats and dogs at every turn. Even if I wanted to hire her I couldn't.

"Because ..." I said, and reached out a hand. My movement so quick and unexpected, she did not have a chance to react. I pulled her towards me and her luscious curves slammed into me. So hard, she gasped, her mouth falling open with astonishment and excitement.

"Of this," I murmured as my mouth crashed down on hers. For at least a whole instant she remained so shocked she was frozen, then she began to struggle. I didn't let go. I waited for the natural desire between us to burst into flames.

And it did.

Unfortunately, it was not what I thought it would be.

It was not a fire, it was a volcano that erupted. We devoured each other, my hands slipped to her ass and squeezed. It was a fine ass. I could already see it bare. I could tell she was completely lost. I could have taken her right there on my desk. And I would have if I did not have the urgent problem of finding a nanny for little Yulia. No, I'll save this flower for later. I lifted my head and looked into her eyes. They were half-dazed with lust.

She blinked. Once, twice, thrice.

Then she made her own move. She stepped back and swung her arm forward and caught my cheek in a stinging slap. It would have galled her to know, I could have stopped her hand at any time from the moment she decided to do it, but I wanted to feel the violence I had aroused in her. It felt good to see her face become pale when she realized what she had done. No one had ever caused her to lose control in that way before.

I smiled.

She stared at me in disbelief then she turned on her heel and walked quickly out of the door. She didn't bother to close the door so I watched her ramrod straight back as she crossed the music room. As she got halfway down the room I saw a small figure slip out from behind the heavy curtains and approach her. The affronted nanny came to a sudden stop. As I watched in amazement, my niece curled her hand around April Winter's middle finger.

Oh fuck!

To be continued...

GREAT NEWS!
For those of you who just can't wait you can pre-order Nanny & The Beast here:
Amazon

ABOUT THE AUTHOR

Discover more information about Georgia Le Carre and
future releases here.
https://www.facebook.com/georgia.lecarre
https://twitter.com/georgiaLeCarre
http://www.goodreads.com/GeorgiaLeCarre
https://www.amazon.com/Georgia-Le-
Carre/e/B00FXN8N0S

Printed in Great Britain
by Amazon